"I don't like it. I don't want Mom to get sick again." Jane takes a spoon and starts cutting up her toast into little, curved, buttery pieces. She's making a mess all over the table, but Dad doesn't say anything about it.

"Of course you don't like it," Dad says. "Liza and I don't like it, either. And neither does Mom. But after all this is over, she's going to be healthier than she was before." Dad reaches out and touches Jane's hand, and the spoon slips out of it. "It's going to be all right, Janie."

Jane jerks her hand back. "People die from cancer." She sounds angry. Why's she so angry at Dad? It isn't his fault. "They die all the time from cancer. A girl at my school—Suzanne Thatcher—her mother died from breast cancer last year. And that's what Mom has. Breast cancer. She might die from it."

Both Sides Now

Ruth Pennebaker

LAUREL-LEAF BOOKS

I want to thank Mary Winsett, M.D., and Owen Winsett, M.D., for reading this manuscript and giving me their expertise and encouragement. I'm also indebted to my wonderful editor, Marc Aronson, who pushed me more than I wanted to be pushed on this book, and to my superb agent, Lois Wallace. Thanks, too, to my family and friends for putting up with me. This hasn't been an easy book for any of us.

Published by
Dell Laurel-Leaf
an imprint of
Random House Children's Books
a division of Random House, Inc.
1540 Broadway
New York, New York 10036

Visit us on the Web! www.randomhouse.com/teens

Educators and librarians, for a variety of teaching tools, visit us at www.randomhouse.com/teachers

ISBN: 0-440-22933-2

RL: 5.3

Reprinted by arrangement with Henry Holt and Company, LLC

Printed in the United States of America

July 2002

10 9 8 7 6 5 4 3 2 1

OPM

For Ellen
and for the memory of our mother

Both Sides Now

It's foggy and misty this morning, but I can see the finish line the minute I turn the last corner. It's about a block away. Lots of people are standing around it, clapping and yelling. There are pink balloons everywhere, and they bob up and down in the wind.

When I cross the line, a woman in a white sweatshirt and aviator glasses gives me a big pink button that says *I Raced for the Cure!* I pin it on my T-shirt while I'm still jogging up and down. I look around, but I don't see Mom anywhere.

So I turn back and jog along the sidewalk, watching all the people who are still finishing the race. At first, they're all runners like me—young kids, college students, middle-aged guys with babies on their backs. But the farther back I go, the slower people are moving. After I've gone four or five blocks, you couldn't even call it a race. It's like a party that's walking very slowly. There are mostly women in long, wavy lines with their friends. They're talking and laughing and pushing strollers.

Mom and her friends are almost at the end of the crowd. She's with three women from her support group. They're all wearing pink T-shirts and visors that say *I'm a breast cancer survivor!*

"Liza!" Mom's waving at me. I jog over next to her and slow down to walk with her and her friends.

"You remember my older daughter, Liza?" Mom asks the other

women. She pushes her hair back when she talks, the way she always has. Mom has a very pretty face, with deep blue eyes and soft skin and short, dark brown hair. Even though she doesn't like to exercise that much, she looks happy today. "Liza's a runner—when she's not doing lots of other things. She's the real achiever in the family."

The other women and I smile at one another and nod. I've met all of them before. There's Barbara, who's short and peppy and probably the most cheerful-looking person I've ever met in my life. She almost always has lipstick on her teeth from smiling so much. Then there's Jeannette, who's taller and more serious, and Libby, who has pale skin and big brown eyes.

The three of them have very short hair, like Mom's. That's because they all had breast cancer and went through chemotherapy a few months ago.

When Mom and the other women talk about chemotherapy, they call it "chemo," for short. I think it helps to give something a nickname like that, so it doesn't sound as scary. Besides, chemo isn't as bad as most people think. It kills the cancer cells in your body and saves your life. That's what you have to keep telling yourself.

"You think we'll win the race, Liza?" Barbara asks. She winks at me, and Mom and all her friends start laughing. Right now, the five of us are walking so slowly that it's going to take a year to finish. They might have taken the finish line down and gone home by the time we get there.

About ten minutes later, we turn the final corner. The finish line is still there, with all the pink balloons flapping around. By now, it's gotten hotter, and the fog and mist have disappeared. The sun is shining, bright and golden and beautiful, and you can see the soft green hills in the distance. That's a good sign. I always look for good signs, and I almost always find them, too. It's amazing.

People are yelling when we cross the line. I think it's because

4

we're practically the last people to finish the race. Mom and her friends hug each other, and they all hug me.

Around us, all I can see is a small crowd of women wearing pink. They move together and apart and together again, and their faces look hot and red from the sun. They're laughing and crying at the same time, in a way that's hard for me to explain. I don't think I've ever seen anything like that before.

I hug Mom again. She's laughing and crying, like the rest of the women. For a few seconds, I don't know what to say.

What should I say? The day's beautiful and we've finished the race and I feel so happy to be alive—like something wonderful's going to happen any minute now. Something wonderful's going to happen, bursting out of nowhere, the way the sun just came out. Everything is going to be all right. It's such a strong feeling, like a surge of something very powerful, that I know it must be true. I wish I could explain it better. I wish I could make Mom and her friends understand. I wish I could make everybody in the world understand.

"Let's go, babe," Mom says. She stretches her arms up, over her head, and grins at me. "I need to get to the closest shower. It's an emergency."

❀❀ ❀❀ ❀❀

I drive us home. I got my learner's permit last summer, and I'm starting driver's ed classes this week, so I need to practice driving as much as I can. The trouble is, I don't have very good depth perception. That's why I have this bad habit of running over curbs. Dad says I shouldn't worry about it, though. It's a bad habit to focus on mistakes, because that's negative. As long as I act like I have confidence in my driving, I'll start to feel it, he says.

I don't think Mom agrees, though. She gets a little nervous when I run over curbs, so I try not to do it as much when she's in the car with me.

I push hard on the accelerator, so I can get out of the parking lot and into the flow of traffic quickly. The car jumps out of the parking lot, then it fishtails on the street.

"My God, Liza," Mom says. "Slow down. Who taught you to drive like that?"

I yank my foot off the accelerator. The car almost lurches to a stop. Uh-oh. That reminds me of what Dad said the last time we went out driving. I need to work on *smoothness*. "Well—Dad's been teaching me. He says the biggest mistake new drivers make is being too cautious."

Mom leans her head back against the seat and makes a noise that sounds like a snort. "I hadn't realized cautiousness was such a bad habit."

She sounds grumpy. So I continue to drive slowly, more like Mom does, so she won't get upset with me. We creep along the street like a big metal turtle, and cars whiz past us.

The only people we pass are bicyclists and joggers along the side of the road. The bicyclists are dressed in bright-colored, skintight clothes, and they're wearing helmets and movie-star sunglasses. They look serious. The joggers are wearing baggy T-shirts and shorts that don't match. They don't look nearly as serious as the bicyclists, and they're very sweaty and they're mopping their faces with towels. I like the joggers a lot more than I like the bicyclists, even though they're not nearly as glamorous.

Since the day's turned out to be pretty, the whole hike-and-bike trail is crowded. The trail runs along both sides of the river, and you can see people with dogs and little kids, just loping along, moving in and out of the trees. There are a few boats on the river, sliding

6

along the smooth blue water. We live in Austin, and the summer lasts about six months, unless it's a really hot year. But once we get past all those hundred-degree days, everyone leaves their houses and air conditioners and comes outside. Like today. It's November, and the weather's gorgeous.

We pass over the expressway and into our neighborhood in West Austin. The streets curve around, up and down hills, and trees stretch over the middle of the road. It's a funny area, with big and small houses, older homes and new ones made from limestone. Some of the houses have beautiful green lawns, and others are overgrown with cactus and brush and prickly pear. A few people have swings and slides in their front yard, and there are children running down the streets yelling and laughing. It's a casual, mixed kind of neighborhood, and I love it. I've lived here my whole life.

Our house is a two-story, made out of painted white brick, with black shutters. In the flower beds in front of the shrubs, there are yellow and purple pansies with markings that look like funny little faces. My best friend, Rory, says we live in a real *Leave It to Beaver* kind of house. Every time she comes over, she says, she's surprised not to see a woman in a full skirt and apron and pearls, pulling cookies out of the oven. "You know—one of those dippy, happy homemakers that make you want to gag," she says. "Not like your mom at all."

I pull into our driveway and press the automatic garage door opener. I hope Mom notices that I park the car perfectly in the garage and don't hit any of the bicycles or sacks of fertilizer along the wall, the way I did last week. I'm definitely getting better at this.

Inside, Dad's at the counter in the kitchen, drinking black coffee and reading the newspapers. He's very tall and thin. When I was a little kid, I used to think he looked like a praying mantis with a lot of energy. He has very dark, lively eyes, and his hair's going gray and it's thinner than it used to be. As usual, it's sticking straight up in the air. But he looks cheerful, the way he always does.

"My two favorite women," he says. He has a very deep, booming voice. He kisses Mom on the cheek, then me. He hasn't shaved yet, and his face feels like a cactus. "How was the race?"

"It was great," I say. "We had a lot of fun. The weather was perfect."

"We had a wonderful crowd," Mom says. "I'm sure we raised lots of money. Next year, you and Jane need to come with us, Will." She sits down at the counter, two stools away from Dad, and props her chin on her hands. "I'm a complete sweatball. Don't get too close to me."

"You're a beautiful sweatball," Dad says. He talks to Mom like that all the time. It's kind of embarrassing to be around them.

"Does anybody want orange juice?" I ask. I pour myself a big glass, then I spread some cream cheese on a bagel. I always get very hungry after I've been running. I usually eat standing up, since I'm so busy. I cram the bagel into my mouth and finish my orange juice. I've already had breakfast, and it's too early for lunch. I guess this is a snack.

Then I make myself a big cup of coffee. If you dump in lots of milk and sugar, it tastes like a warm milk shake. That's how I'm learning to drink it. All my friends are going to coffeehouses, and if you order a Coke in one of those places, you look very juvenile. I think it helps to practice at home so you don't spew coffee all over the place the first time you try it.

"Just think," Dad's saying, "one of these days, we're going to find a cure for cancer—and you won't have to have these races." He puts his hands behind his head, with his elbows sticking out, and leans back on the bar stool and smiles. "This is such an exciting time—with all these medical breakthroughs going on."

8

Dad's a pulmonologist—a lung doctor—so he knows a lot about science. He loves science, and so do I. I'm thinking about being a doctor when I grow up, too. I like to help people, and that's what doctors do. They make people's lives better.

Mom shrugs. "If they're going to cure cancer, I wish they'd work a little faster. I'd rather sleep late than go to a race any day." She clears her throat. "Will someone get me some orange juice?"

Dad jumps off the stool and opens the cupboard. "Coming up," he says, pulling out a glass.

"I've got to go. I've got work to do," I say. "I can't sit around like the two of you."

That's supposed to be funny, since Dad's never sat around more than two seconds in his whole life. I think my sense of humor's improving, but sometimes people don't understand my jokes. For example, Mom doesn't even smile when I say that. But Dad does. He gives me a big cheerful grin. He always gets my jokes.

❦ ❦ ❦

After I take a shower upstairs, I get into a bathrobe and head to my room. I used to have a very messy room, but now I've become much more organized. You can get a lot more done when you're organized and you don't spend half your life tripping over piles of clothes and CDs and books.

Besides, Dad and I just painted my room a few weeks ago, and I love the way it looks. It's a very bright yellow—"Matisse yellow" is what it's called. When the sun's coming in through the windows, the whole room is so loud and alive that it makes you blink. Mom says I should hand out sunglasses to anybody who comes into my room. The color's so bright, it gives her a migraine, she says.

I curl up on my bed and drink my coffee very slowly. I must

have made it too strong, because it's a dark tan color. But that's good. My goal is to drink completely black coffee by next fall, when I'm a junior. I probably need to push myself more.

Next year, I'll also have to start thinking about essays to write for college applications. That's kind of a problem. I want to go to a very good school—like Stanford. That's where Dad went to undergraduate and med school. It's one of the best universities in the country.

But I'm not sure what I should write an essay about. Most of the really good schools want you to write very dark, intense, dramatic essays about your life.

The trouble is, I can't think of anything dark and intense and dramatic about my life. Should I make up something? Or should I tell the truth—that I'm a very happy person and I've got a good life?

I mean, I love my parents and my sister, Jane—even though Jane gets on my nerves sometimes, since she's twelve and she's going through adolescence. We have a nice house and enough money so we don't have to worry. I go to a good high school and I'm on the honor roll every six weeks, and I have lots of friends and I'm an officer in my sophomore class. You see what I mean? I've got a great life—but it wouldn't make a great college essay.

Last year, Mom was diagnosed with breast cancer, and I know a lot of people think that's very depressing and dark and intense and dramatic. But it's not, really. Dad's talked a lot to Jane and me about it—about how something like this will make our family stronger. Mom's gone through some tough treatments, but she's all right now. She's healthier and stronger than she's ever been. Cancer used to be incurable, but now it's a highly treatable disease.

We can choose to look at this as something terrible. Or we can look at it as something that's going to make us stronger, better people. That's what

Dad says, and I know he's right. We have piles and piles of books and tapes that say the same thing. They helped us a lot when Mom was sick. Even when we were all feeling bad, they made us see things differently.

Maybe that's what I'll write about next year. I'll write about how difficult things that happen to you can actually make you a better person and help you have a better life. What's important is how you look at the things that happen to you and what you do with them.

I write those sentences down in my journal. I like the way they sound. I think a lot of people might like to read something like that. Even people on admissions committees.

I know I'll have to work really hard to come up with a good college essay. But I'm sure I can do it. I'm good at something like that—work, I mean. I work harder than anyone else I know.

❧❧❧ ❧❧❧ ❧❧❧

"Oh, my God, Liza. Wait till I tell you about my weekend. I'm in *love*."

That's my best friend, Rory Chambliss, talking. She tosses her hair over her shoulder, and a big wave of her perfume hits me. Rory falls in love almost every weekend, and it usually lasts till Thursday.

We're in first-period honors French II together, and we sit catty-corner from each other. I think that's a good distance. If we sat closer together, Rory would probably be talking to me all the time and I wouldn't learn any French, ever. All I'd know about is sex. That would be interesting, I guess, but it's not going to be on anybody's six-week test and end up on my transcript. It's not even an extracurricular activity, even though Rory sometimes acts like it is.

All of a sudden, Rory sits up straight, like she's in the military. She starts gesturing to me and pointing to the front of the classroom.

"Look at him," she whispers loudly. "*Jesus Cristo.* Holy shit. He's a vision. How'm I supposed to concentrate with guys like that around?" She draws in her breath loudly. "It's hopeless. There goes my GPA."

If you want to know the truth, Rory's GPA went Deep South a long time ago. She's one of the smartest people I've ever known in my life, but she's practically flunking out of school. Also, you'd never realize she was smart by looking at her. Ever since we started high school, she's been dressing in very tight tops and short skirts, and pants that look like someone painted them on her. It must be very hard to breathe in the clothes she wears. I said that to her one time, as kind of a joke. Rory said there were lots of things that were more important than breathing.

"Look at him," she whispers again.

I turn around to face the front of the room. *There.* That must be who she's talking about. He's almost as tall as my father, and he's talking to Ms. Reynolds, our teacher. He has dark brown hair and eyes, and he's wearing a forest green shirt with short sleeves. His arms are tan and long, and when he moves them, I can see his muscles shift.

Ms. Reynolds points to a seat in the back of the room, and the guy walks down the aisle between Rory and me. For just a second, while he passes, our eyes meet. I feel dizzy for some reason.

He keeps walking, and Rory turns around and cranes her neck at him and points right at his butt. When she sees me looking at her, she whistles softly and shakes her head. "I love these Romance languages," she says in a loud whisper. Everyone around us starts to laugh.

I swivel around in my seat and try to pay attention to Ms. Reynolds. That's hard. She has hair that looks like platinum cotton candy, and big blue eyes, and she wears lots of sky-blue eye shadow all over her lids. The truth is, she looks like one of those country-and-western singers, except she doesn't wear clothes that are sparkly enough. She has the reputation for being the worst teacher in our whole high school. Rory says she thinks Ms. Reynolds tries to make up for being such a horrible teacher by having interesting hair.

"She takes great care of it," Rory said once. "I've never seen her roots—not once—and believe me, I've looked. Her hair is a work of art, Liza. That's it. Sure, a French poodle speaks more French than Ms. Reynolds. But so what? Her hair is her passion—her *life*." Rory's always saying dramatic things like that. She's a very interesting person. If I ever want to write a book, I think I'll just follow Rory around and write down everything she says.

But I still wish Ms. Reynolds would find more passion for French than her hair one of these days. She has the worst accent I've ever heard. I've been to Paris with my family, and my French is a lot better than hers. I don't think Ms. Reynolds has ever been anywhere but Paris, Texas. So I try not to listen to her pronounce anything. I'd hate to start sounding like her. Now that I think about it, she speaks French kind of like a country-and-western singer, too. If LeAnn Rimes took up French, she'd sound a lot like Ms. Reynolds.

Right now, Ms. Reynolds is standing in front of the class, trying to teach. She's short and plump under all that hair, and she spends most of her time gesturing with her hands when she can't think of the right words to say. Sometimes, she looks like she's teaching a class in sign language or cheerleading. Today's one of those days.

I can feel my mind drift. I'm almost always good about paying attention in class, but I don't feel like watching Ms. Reynolds do a bunch of calisthenics in front of the blackboard. It's too frustrating.

Maybe I should go to see the school counselor and ask if I can transfer to another French class so I can learn something for a change. But I'd never do anything like that. I wouldn't want to hurt Ms. Reynolds's career, even if she isn't very good at it. Maybe I could just say we have a personality conflict. That would make it sound like it was my fault, too.

I sit and draw things with my pencil—big flowers and lightning bolts and two-story houses with trees growing out of them. Rory's trying to get my attention. I can see her out of the corner of my eye, but I pretend I don't. She'd pass notes back and forth to me and mouth comments all the time, if I'd let her. But I don't want to.

Besides, I talk to Rory on the phone almost every day. Sometimes, she comes to my house, but I almost never go to hers. She lives with her mother and stepfather in a tiny house in Clarksville. That's kind of an ex-hippie area close to downtown. Some of the houses are big and wonderful, and some of them are really rundown. Rory lives in a house that looks like it's about to collapse. It's light pink, but most of the paint is peeling, and it slants over to one side, like it needs to be propped up. I don't know if it bothers Rory or not. That might be why she never wants me to come over to her house. But it could also be because she hates her stepfather so much. His name is Jonah. He has long, greasy gray hair, and he's a choir director at some church, but he also plays the steel guitar in a rock band. Rory says she's heard a lot of really bad bands in Austin, but her stepfather's is the worst. They're like a bunch of deaf Stevie Wonders, she says, except they're not black and they don't have any talent.

Finally, after about several million years and two irregular verbs Ms. Reynolds can't remember, the bell rings. We all jump up and head out the door, like we're a bunch of horses in the starting gate

14

and we want to beat everybody else. Ms. Reynolds looks as happy as the rest of us. Even happier, maybe. *"A bientôt!"* she says.

Rory clutches my elbow while we walk out the door. "I feel much more interested in French after today," she whispers. "God, that new guy is gorgeous. I'd *love* to conjugate some irregular verbs with him."

We step out into the hall, and the new guy walks past us. He turns and looks right at me again. His eyes are dark, dark brown, and there's something soft and sweet about them, something that makes me lean toward him for just a few seconds.

Rory sees it all, because she always sees things like that. Even when things don't happen, she sees them. When the guy disappears into the hallway, she nudges me and starts to laugh. "Liza, Liza, Liza. Oh, sweetie, you should *see* your face."

❧❧❧ ❧❧❧ ❧❧❧

Our high-school cafeteria is so loud that sometimes you have to scream so people at the same table can hear you. That's what we're doing today, screaming. I'm sitting with Rory and Emma Schwartz and Beverly Proctor, and we're complaining about the food, the way we always do.

"Look at *this*," Emma's saying in a loud voice. She pokes at something that's supposed to be spinach casserole. The cheese has kind of decomposed, and there's a lot of orange liquid on the plate around it. *"Prisons* have better food than this. They put people in maximum-security units and punish them with slop like this. This is what they serve inmates on death row, so they won't mind dying so much."

Emma makes a face, then she grins at us. She has chin-length black hair and gorgeous white teeth, almost like a movie star's. Rory says Emma has great teeth because her father's an orthodontist, and orthodontists won't let their kids out of the house if they don't have beautiful teeth. Otherwise, it would be very bad for business. Rory claims that Emma's had all her teeth capped so Dr. Schwartz will get lots more patients. I'm not sure it's true, though. Sometimes Rory says things that aren't true, just because they sound funny.

Emma and Beverly and Rory and I have been friends since we were in grade school. I guess it's because we're so much alike. We make good grades and we're involved in lots of activities and we laugh at the same things and we're all going to college. Our pasts are alike and so are our futures. Lots of times, it's easier to be friends with people you don't have to explain everything to. I guess that's it.

What I really mean is that we all *used* to be alike. Rory's changed a lot since we got to high school, but the other three of us haven't. Besides the way she dresses, she's had lots and lots of boyfriends, and she likes to talk and joke about sex all the time. I mean, *constantly*. I guess it was coming to high school that made her change. Either that, or her mother's getting married to Jonah. That happened at about the same time we started high school. I don't know what it was, exactly, but Rory looks different and she acts different.

That makes Beverly and Emma mad. I'm not sure why. I guess I could ask them, but I don't want to.

Besides, I don't think Rory's changed as much as they think. To me, she's still the same person I've always known. When I look at her, I can still see her when she was five and knocked out her front tooth when she fell off a bicycle. Or when she sold more cookies than any other Girl Scout when we were in the sixth grade, and got

16

her picture in the newspaper. She's always been funny and crazy and a little wild.

She hasn't changed—not really. She just *looks* like she's changed. The way she dresses and swears all the time doesn't have anything to do with who she is. Rory's always been my friend, and she always will be. I don't care what she does or what other people think of her. I just don't want her to hurt herself. Sometimes I worry about that.

"I can't eat food this awful," Beverly says. She pushes her tray to the middle of the table and crosses her arms and tosses her hair back.

Beverly has curly dark brown hair and dark eyes, and she's very pretty. Ever since we got to high school, she looks more and more like her mom. I don't know what it is, exactly. It's like she's really happy with herself. Maybe a little too happy.

Mrs. Proctor is one of those West Austin moms everybody talks about. She drives around in a Suburban and plays tennis at the country club and runs the PTA. She hangs around the high school almost as much as we do. One time, Mom said that Mrs. Proctor had too much time on her hands. I don't think she likes Mrs. Proctor.

Rory hates Mrs. Proctor and Beverly, and I know that because she's told me about three hundred times. She gets upset because Mrs. Proctor doesn't approve of her—that's what it really is. Mrs. Proctor says that Rory's boy-crazy, and she makes that sound like a disease. Beverly says her mother doesn't dislike Rory. She just feels sorry for her, since Rory and her mother are both such tramps.

I've heard Mrs. Proctor say that plenty of times, but I'm not sure I believe she's sorry about anything. She has a funny way of saying things in a very sweet voice—but there's something wrong with it. She sounds nice, and she says she's sorry, but she isn't. Not really.

"How was *your* weekend, Liza?" Emma asks. She's stopped complaining about the spinach casserole, and now she's eating it. She grins at me. "Got anybody new on the line?"

I shrug and say no. Not yet. "It was a pretty quiet weekend. I studied a lot."

Oh, please. People at this high school are very, very concerned about who you're dating. It's a big deal, even though I think it's immature.

Emma and Beverly have both been dating the same guys since middle school, Jay Thomas and Andrew McLemore. Jay plays basketball and Andrew's on the football team, and they're popular and good-looking. I haven't gone out with anyone since I broke up with Ed Baird a couple of weeks ago. He was a really nice guy, but I felt like he was a little too serious about me. That made me uncomfortable. I think it's great to date a lot in high school, but I don't think you should get *serious* about anyone.

"It never takes Liza too long to come up with somebody new," Rory says loudly. "I give her another ten minutes. She was *stricken* with this new guy in our French class."

I can tell Rory's dying for Beverly and Emma to ask who she's dating now. But they won't do it. They never do. They always ask me who Rory's going out with, but they'd never ask *her* in a million years. They'd never give her the satisfaction, that's what Beverly says. "I don't want Rory to think we're that interested in her life—because we're not."

But they are. Beverly and Emma are extremely interested in Rory's life. It's just that they don't like her any longer, and sometimes I wonder what I'm going to do about that. Maybe it will get better—that's what I've been telling myself for a long time. But it hasn't. Sometimes I think it's getting worse.

I crumple my napkin and drop it on my plate. My plate's clean, like I almost licked it or something. That's how you have to learn to eat in our school cafeteria. You don't notice that the food's terrible if you eat it really, really quickly.

After school's over, I stop by the rest room so I can put on some lipstick and comb my hair. I have dark blond hair that's the same color Dad's used to be before it started falling out all over the place. I'm pretty sure my hair is my best feature. That's what all my friends say, anyway.

I try not to think about things like my appearance, though. That can make you really superficial. Some of the girls I know just think about how they look all the time and about the boys they date and how many kids they're going to have someday. They don't think about their future enough, and they don't plan for anything. If you don't plan, you'll get taken by surprise, and I don't want that to happen to me. I want to plan for everything so I can have a good, successful life. If you're going to accomplish something, you need to start as early as possible. That's what Dad says, and he knows what he's talking about. He says we can all control our own destinies— but we have to work at it.

This year, I'm a reporter for the school newspaper, the *Houston High Herald*. I don't think I want to go into journalism, but I spend lots of time working for the paper. Right now, I need to go to the journalism room and finish my advice column. The column's called "Dear Deborah," and it's been in our school newspaper since the 1970s, so it's practically an institution. I've got to answer three letters before I go home today.

A girl named Deborah Ames started this column in 1976, and everybody made fun of it. Deborah was always giving serious answers to phony questions people sent in, such as whether you could get pregnant from an empty Coke bottle or whether it had to be full. All the kids in the school thought it was a great big joke, and they used to send in worse and worse letters. But Deborah would always answer every one of them like they were serious. She must have been one of those people who didn't have a good sense of humor.

In fact, the whole column was so awful that it probably would have been dumped after Deborah graduated that year. But she didn't. About a month before commencement, she was driving on the highway, and a big tractor-trailer ran over her. She was in a little yellow Volkswagen Bug, and they had to spend three or four hours getting her body out of the wreck. Some photographers stopped by and took a bunch of pictures. One of them was in the school newspaper. It showed Deborah's car crumpled up, and all you could see of her was one hand sticking out of the window. It was a terrible picture, but I think it won some kind of national prize or something.

After that, everybody in the whole senior class—especially the kids who'd written phony letters to Deborah—felt terrible about how mean they'd been to her. They dedicated all the senior-class money to an endowment fund so the column would stay in the school newspaper to honor Deborah. Everybody forgot that the column had been terrible and that none of them had liked Deborah anyway. It was very strange. I guess that when people get upset about something, they do all sorts of weird things. The last few weeks of school, they had car washes and bake sales to make money for the fund, and somebody even painted a portrait of Deborah for the journalism room.

The portrait's still there, hanging on top of the blackboard in the front of the room. It's the first thing you see when you walk in. Deborah had long dark hair and great big black eyes. She must have had some sort of Frida Kahlo fixation, because she had only one long eyebrow over both her eyes, and she looked like she knew something tragic was going to happen to her. Or maybe the painter got bored and just decided to paint Frida Kahlo, instead.

Every year since then, they've chosen a student to write the "Dear Deborah" column. The funny thing is, it's become a big honor, and it's really competitive. Last year, there were twenty-two other kids who tried out. We had to answer all kinds of different questions to see how we'd handle the answers and how empathetic we were. Empathy is extremely important—that's what Mr. Sorensen, our journalism teacher, says.

Mr. Sorensen said he chose me last spring to write the column because I was the most level-headed freshman he'd ever met in his life. He said that as far as he could tell, I was quite well-adjusted and maybe I could help other students be happier and more directed, the way I am. I felt embarrassed when he told me that. But it made me feel good, too. "You're the kind of person everybody else can rely on," Mr. Sorensen said. He said that was a very big compliment to my maturity.

I'd die if anybody knew how seriously I take this column. The truth is, I spend a lot of time on it. If I give the right answers, then maybe I can make a difference in other people's lives. But most kids in high school act like you're not supposed to take anything that seriously. So I never talk much about the column. It's kind of a private part of my life, even though it's in the newspaper.

Once I get to the journalism room, I sit at a desk that faces the wall and spread out all the letters I've gotten. I keep the letters in a big padded manila envelope that says *Dear Deborah Column. Private. Keep Out!* That's so Jane won't go nosing around in them. She's so immature that she doesn't realize all the letters I get are highly confidential. I can just see her reading some of the letters and talking to her childish friends about them. That would be very typical. Second

21

children don't grow up nearly as quickly as older kids do. I read that somewhere, and believe me, Jane is living proof of that.

Fortunately, no one else is in the newspaper room today, and it's quiet. That's good. I can work a lot better when no one's trying to talk to me.

One of the hardest things about this column is picking out which letters to use. What if there are kids out there who really need advice—but I don't pick their letters? Then what are they going to do? I want to make sure I pick out the letters that need good answers, and then I work a long time to write the best answers I can come up with.

Most of the letters are written on notebook paper that's been torn out, and they're jagged along the edges. Sometimes, whoever's written a letter puts so much pressure on the pen that they tear the paper. I don't know what that means, exactly, but it must be important.

This month, I have a letter from a girl who gets sick to her stomach every time she thinks about food. Then there's a note from a boy who promised his parents he wouldn't drink anymore. But now he's depressed because his girlfriend broke up with him, and he really needs to drink.

After I've read through all the notes, I decide to answer their two letters, and one that's signed, "Jeff." He wrote, *Dear Deborah: I want to get into a good college, but I also like to party a lot. Are there any colleges for people who like to groove?*

I bet Jeff isn't his real name. I wonder if he's joking. But even if he is, there might be something serious about his question. Sometimes, you try to joke about things that are really important to you. Like me. I joke about getting into Stanford, because I want to go there so much. When you do something like that, you feel like you're kind of protecting yourself so you won't get too disappointed. Maybe that's what Jeff's doing. Maybe he's one of those faculty kids from the University of Texas whose father won a Nobel Prize or something, and he knows he's never going to do that much with his life. Things like that happen a lot at our high school. It's very competitive when you're on the honors track.

Anyway, that's what I do the rest of the afternoon. I type Jeff's letter into the computer, along with the other two. I think that's a pretty good ratio of two very serious letters and one that isn't quite so serious. I tell the girl who can't eat and the boy who wants to drink that they should seek professional help immediately. I know that sounds like I'm avoiding the issue, but I don't want them to think I'm a professional counselor when I'm not.

I try to make Jeff's answer light and breezy, the way Mr. Sorensen says I should. He says if everything's too serious, no one will pay much attention to the column. *Dear Jeff: We all love parties, especially after we've been studying hard. But remember how important college is to your future. If you go to a good college, then you'll have more time and money to party for the rest of your life.*

There. That's a good answer. Maybe it will help Jeff look at some of the choices he's making right now. We all have choices— that's what the self-help books say. Even when we don't do anything, we're making a choice. It's very important to remember that.

I proofread my answers, then I save the file and send it to Mr. Sorensen's computer. Then I stretch and yawn. I'm kind of tired. It takes a lot of energy to try to help other people.

Most of the time, I write the column while I'm at home, instead of in the journalism room. I guess it sounds silly, but sometimes it's hard for me to work at school. Deborah's picture is right there, beside the blackboard, and sometimes I feel like I can't concentrate when I'm in the same room with it.

I look up and see her black eyes staring at me. They make me feel nervous, like I'm missing something important and I'm not as good as I think I am. That's dumb, I know. It's crazy! Besides, why should I care? Deborah wrote terrible advice when she was alive.

So I don't even know why it matters to me. But sometimes, when I look up and see Deborah's face, I feel like she's disappointed in me. She's staring at me with that same sad look in her eyes. Even after I look down, I can still see her face. Sometimes I feel like she's trying to tell me something I don't want to know.

Will is at work, and the girls are in school now. So the house is quiet. It's lonely, but it's easier for me to think.

There are days when I feel exhausted, just being around the three of them. They all want so much from me—especially Will and Liza. Sometimes, I'm almost relieved when they drive off and leave me alone.

For so many years, they've wanted me to be different. They love me, but they want me to be someone I'm not. That's what breaks my heart. They want me to be someone who's better—someone who's strong and positive and confident—and I can't be that person.

After all these years, I can "see" this woman I should be too damned clearly. She's prettier than I am, and she doesn't have any of those knobby little varicose veins I've gotten. She's a natural blond with a great big smile, someone who strides through life. If she stumbles at all, she picks herself up and goes on. She's successful and extroverted, fun-loving, the life of every goddamn party she goes to.

I hate her, of course. I hate her almost as much as I want to be exactly like her.

But I'm not. I know who I really am, no matter how hard I try. A woman with a sad, worried look on her face, who's always trying to please.

She's depressed and hopeless and scared to death about her future. She's terrified about what this week will bring.

I hate that woman, too. I've hated her for years.

Sometimes, I want to tell Liza and Jane to grow up and be better and stronger and freer than I am. Don't be depressed and afraid of life. Don't be like me, for God's sake!

But then I look at Liza more closely. I realize she already understands that.

Tuesday after school, Mom and I go to the driver's ed school. It's about a mile from our high school, close to the natural-foods market.

Mom's not very talkative today. She's sitting in the seat next to me while I drive, and sometimes she runs her hand through her hair and sighs. I don't think she's sighing about my driving, but you never know. I wish I could ask her, but I don't think I should. It might ruin my confidence in my driving if she thinks I'm a really terrible driver. If I'm going to take driver's ed, I need lots of confidence.

We head down Fifth Street, past the enormous tree that's called Treaty Oak. It's about the size of a building. The tree's very famous, because someone signed a treaty there a long time ago. It had something to do with the Texas Revolution, I think.

A few years ago, the tree started dying. Its leaves turned brown and dropped off. Every day, there were pictures and stories about it in the Austin newspaper. An expert on oak trees came to look at it. He said that somebody was deliberately poisoning the tree, which shocked everybody in the whole town. People started holding nighttime candlelight vigils around the tree, and they left signs and get-well cards on the grass around it.

Also, lots of people wrote letters to the editor of the newspaper to say they couldn't believe someone would poison such a beautiful, historic tree. *I thought humanity had sunk to its lowest when our animal shelters started killing puppies and kittens,* someone wrote. *But now I realize that was only the beginning. I've tried and tried to think how someone—anyone!—could be sick and perverted enough to kill an innocent tree. But I've come up with no answers.* The person who wrote that letter also suggested that if all those Right to Life people really cared about other beings, they should be out in front of Treaty Oak, demonstrating for the rights of plants to live, instead of hanging around abortion clinics all the time.

Other people wrote letters to the editor saying that Treaty Oak had started dying at exactly the same time lots of high-tech people from California and a bunch of Yankees all moved here. *Is this a coincidence?* someone wrote. *I don't think so.*

People who've lived in Austin a long time are always saying things like that. Austin's a really great place to live, with lots of music and rolling hills and big trees. It's a very liberal city, especially for Texas. You can see lots of old hippies around here who are about my parents' age. Dad says they're still probably wearing the same blue jeans they wore in 1968. Downtown, on Congress Avenue, a homeless guy named Ralph lives right on the street. He has long blond hair and wears lots of eye makeup and lipstick. Most of the time, he dresses in a pink tutu and carries a parasol. I think he's a transsexual. You wouldn't find somebody like Ralph in any other Texas city, except for Austin. That's what people here say.

But now everybody's complaining about how big Austin's gotten and how bad the traffic is and how much it's changing. I think about a thousand new people move here every day. Or maybe it's five thousand. Anyway, it's a lot. Everybody says Austin used to be perfect twenty or thirty years ago, and now it's going straight to hell in a handbasket. Some of the new people who've moved here drive luxury cars and vote Republican, which is extremely embarrassing to people who've been here a long time. A few weeks ago, some of the downtown business owners wanted to run off Ralph, because they said he was bad for business. There were lots of letters to the editor about that, too. People here love to write letters to the editor. Most of them said that all these newcomers wanted to make Austin bland, just like Dallas and Houston. In fact, Ralph was a *symbol* of Austin, some of them said.

I guess Austin's changed a lot, since everybody says it has. But I'm kind of tired of hearing about it. It's very boring to hear the same thing over and over. Besides, Treaty Oak survived just fine. They sawed off a few branches, and now it looks lopsided. But at least it's still alive. I guess whoever was poisoning it was scared off by all the candlelight vigils. And the last time I was downtown, I saw Ralph, as usual. He was wearing a yellow net prom dress that day, waving a wand with a star at the end and throwing glitter in the air.

I pull into a parking space. Then I get out of the car, and Mom comes around to the driver's seat. She stands on her tiptoes and kisses me on the top of my head. I grew two or three inches last summer, and now I'm taller than she is. I think it still surprises both of us.

"Your father's picking you up, babe," she says. It's the first thing she's said all afternoon, practically. "Good luck with the driving."

❦❦❦ ❦❦❦ ❦❦❦

I take the elevator to the third floor and walk down the hall past several offices. One of them is for a woman who practices law and teaches yoga. There are also a few acupuncture offices. Lots of Mom's and Dad's friends come here for acupuncture, and they say it makes them feel wonderful. I've never tried it, though. I don't like people sticking needles in me. It doesn't seem safe. That's one reason I'm sure I'll never become a drug addict.

The Driving Safe-T office is at the end of the hall. I came here almost every night last month for all the classroom instruction. The entry room has two dark-green plastic couches and an old coffee table that tilts to the right. It's decorated with pictures of very, very gory wrecks, with cars twisted up till they look like metal basket-balls. In one of them, you can see where three bodies have been covered over with blankets. Underneath all the pictures, there's a sign that shows the date of the wreck and how many people died in it. Teenagers' names and ages are underlined.

That's what this school is famous for—showing teenagers how serious driving is. The school says that if they can keep more teenagers off the roads, then they've done their duty. It's kind of a strange goal for a driving school, if you ask me. They like to brag about how high their dropout rate is.

"You're five minutes late, Liza." That's our driving instruc-tor, Mr. Bridges. He's short and plump, and he wears his hair in a crew cut. Today, he's wearing a maroon sweatshirt that says *Texas A&M*. That's a state university that's about a hundred miles from here, where almost every guy wears a crew cut and marches around all the time.

People in Austin love to tell "Aggie" jokes, about how dumb everybody who goes to A&M is. A lot of the jokes are pretty lame. But ever since I met Mr. Bridges, I've been wanting to tell one of those jokes when he's around. Especially the one about the Aggie with a hundred lovers, which is the only funny Aggie joke I've ever heard in my life. (Here it is: *What do you call an Aggie with a hundred lovers? A shepherd.*)

I usually don't like to tell jokes. I don't think they're funny. But I keep wanting to tell that joke while I'm around Mr. Bridges because I can tell he doesn't like me. I don't know why. It's weird, because my teachers always like me a lot. Almost everyone likes me. But I can tell Mr. Bridges doesn't.

"You're never going to learn to drive safely if you're late"— that's all he says to me, in a very mean voice. He snaps some papers onto a clipboard. "Well, let's get a move on."

He gestures at me and Frank Fuller, who's the other student driver. Frank is supposed to be a junior, but he flunked the ninth grade. He's not in any of my classes, since he's not in the honors track. I hate to sound narrow-minded, because I'm trying to be a tolerant person. But I think Frank is one of those kids who just hang around high school, sharpening their switchblades, till they get older and go to prison. Every time I see him at school, he's talking with guys who look kind of dangerous. They wear black all the time—mostly leather. I think they're in a gang together, but I don't know which one. I hear a lot about gangs, but nobody I know is in one.

"Great outfit, Liza," Frank says. He pulls the corners of his mouth into something that's kind of like a smile, but it looks cold and mean. "You're certainly looking wholesome today."

He grins at me again, like he's just told a dirty joke. I'm wearing a T-shirt and jeans, but maybe next time I'll wrap a blanket around myself. I wish Frank wouldn't look at me like that. He's *leering*—that's what he's doing. I don't like it when anybody leers at me.

The truth is, I don't like being around Frank, period, ever. He

29

makes me feel nervous, the way he talks and stares at me. Also, he's so big that I don't feel as strong when I'm around him. Most of the time, I feel like I can take care of myself and that I'm fine. But when I'm around Frank, I feel different. I feel a little bit scared. I don't know why, because he's never done anything to me, and he's never really said anything bad. But there's just something about him that scares me.

"Ladies first," Mr. Bridges says when he opens the car door. He and Frank chuckle, like he's just said something funny.

I get into the car. It's a bright red Taurus with signs on both sides—*Warning: Inexperienced Driver at the Wheel!* Believe me, it's very embarrassing to drive around in a car that says that.

I fasten my seat belt and pull up the seat so I'm comfortable. I look both ways, then I pull out of the parking lot. I try not to go too fast or too slow. As usual, though, I turn too quickly and run over the curb. The car bounces and thuds on the street. I try to pretend like nothing's happened. Maybe they won't notice that I kind of ran over the curb.

"Jesus Christ!" Mr. Bridges says. "You can't even get out of the parking lot, Liza. How're you ever going to drive on the freeway?"

I straighten the wheel and try to drive like I've got confidence. I made a dumb mistake, but so what? It isn't a big deal. Not really. I just need to forget about it and go on. I can learn from my mistakes—that's what's important. If you don't make mistakes, you never learn anything. Mistakes are good, when you think about it. That almost sounds like a good college essay. I'm going to write it down later.

Usually, it helps me to think about things like that, so I can be more philosophical and optimistic. It makes me feel better. But today, it doesn't work.

From the backseat, Frank is laughing so hard he starts to

30

cough. "Your driving's killing me," he says. Then he starts to laugh again, like he's told another dirty joke. This time, Mr. Bridges laughs, too.

❦ ❦ ❦

The next morning, I get up early and run three miles around the neighborhood. It's cool and dark, and the air smells fresh and sweet. I love getting up this early in the morning, when it's so quiet and beautiful. I run up and down the hills, and pass other joggers and people who are walking their dogs. We all wave at each other and say hello, even though we're panting. This is a very friendly neighborhood.

I'm pretty sure that the guy I see walking his big black dog is the movie star who just moved in a few blocks away. He's tall and thin, and he has a wonderful face with a dark tan and white teeth. He waves at me when we pass each other. I'm almost certain it's him, but I try to act like it's a very normal thing to pass by someone who's famous. I know where he lives, because Rory told me the address. She heard it from a friend of her mother's who's a realtor. Lots of teenage girls drive by his house and honk. I'd never do anything like that, even after I get my driver's license. It would be too immature.

I run along Scenic Drive, which looks out over Lake Austin and all the hills on the other side of the water. There are big new houses up in the hills that look like they've been plopped there, like houses and hotels on a Monopoly board. The water in the lake's turned some kind of silvery blue, and it looks smooth and calm. I stand on a low rock wall and stare at the water and the hills for a few seconds. The lights in all the houses are going off, one by one.

I rest there for a few minutes. I always do, because it's so pretty.

31

Stop and smell the roses—you should always do that for a little while every day. It's important.

I jump off the wall and start back home. When I finally get back to our house, it's a little warmer and the sun's coming up, making the sky a soft yellow. It's beautiful. I always feel so good after I run early in the morning. It's a perfect way to start the day.

After my shower, I come downstairs. Mom's sitting in the kitchen, staring at her coffee, and she's still in her bathrobe. She hasn't combed her hair or put on makeup. I can tell she's in one of her bad moods. She smiles and gives me a kiss on the cheek. But she doesn't say anything, and her eyes are sad. She looks at me, but I'm not sure if she really sees me.

Well, maybe it's not a bad mood, exactly. Just a low one. Mom has lots of moods. It's important for Dad and Jane and me to cheer her up when she gets like this.

I pour myself a cup of coffee with milk. Then I sit down and warm my hands around it. That feels great. I wish I didn't have to drink it. I look at the front page of the newspaper to try to find something interesting to talk about.

Before I can say anything, Mom speaks. "I've got a doctor's appointment this afternoon." She shrugs her shoulders just a little bit, like it's not a big deal to her. But I can tell it is. "It's my very first checkup," she says.

I'd forgotten about the appointment. Mom finished all her treatments—surgery and chemotherapy and radiation—in August. Now she's supposed to see her oncologist every three months. Since she's doing so well, it's just a precaution. That's all.

I smile at Mom and put my hand on hers and squeeze. Her hand is soft, and you can see blue veins that show through it because her skin's so pale. She has to wear hats and lots of sunscreen when she goes outside. She doesn't get tan the way Dad and I do.

"I know you're going to be all right," I say. "You look fine and you feel fine. All the bad stuff is over. We just have to put this all behind us."

We just have to put this all behind us—that's what Dad's been saying for the past few months. Something scary happened to us, but now it's over. We came through it just fine, and we're stronger than we've ever been. Mom was sick a few months ago—but she's fine now. Besides, she's seeing one of the best oncologists in the state, and she's had great medical treatment.

"You're going to be fine," I say again, a little louder. Sometimes, I feel like I'm older than Mom is, like I'm the parent instead of the child.

Mom smiles and nods, but her eyes are still sad. When Dad and Jane and I leave, she waves at us and blows a kiss. That's a good sign. It's a lot better than staring at her coffee.

❧ ❧ ❧

Dad doesn't say much while he drives. Jane's the one who's doing all the talking this morning. I'm pretty sure she didn't used to be this loud. I know she's probably going through a phase or something, but I wish she'd get over it soon.

Jane leans over my shoulder, even though she's in the backseat. She's trying to see herself in the rearview mirror and put on some lipstick. Lipstick! I didn't wear lipstick till I was thirteen, but Jane's already started. Also, her breasts are bigger than mine were when I was her age. If I cared very much about things like that, I'd be very irritated about it.

33

"Guess what we're going to do this afternoon?" she says. "Sarah and I are going to walk by Mac's house. Maybe we'll see him out in his front yard. When he works on his yard, he usually takes off his shirt."

"Mac? Who's Mac?" Dad asks vaguely.

"He's the big movie star who moved into our neighborhood, Dad," Jane says. "I've told you about him a thousand times. Don't you remember anything I tell you?"

She keeps talking about all the movies "Mac" has been in. I've never heard anybody call him Mac before. I wonder where Jane got that. Probably from one of those teenybopper magazines she reads all the time, instead of doing her homework.

Usually, Jane and I get along pretty well. But today, she's driving me nuts. I want to talk to Dad about Mom, and here she is, blabbing about herself and her delusions about some movie star she's never met. I hope I wasn't that bad when I was her age. I'm pretty sure I wasn't. If you want to know the truth, I'll be extremely relieved when Jane gets to be a lot more mature. Like me.

Dad pulls up in front of Jane's school. It's called Crockett Middle School. When I went there two years ago, it looked a lot better than it does now. It's yellow brick and kind of dumpy-looking. Jane thinks it's beautiful, of course. Like most of the schools around here, it's named after someone who died at the Alamo. I don't know what they'd name schools if so many people hadn't died in the Texas Revolution.

"Liza—how does my hair look?" Jane says. She's preening, if you ask me. She already knows her hair looks great. It always does. It's thick and red and gorgeous. Today, she's wearing it in a ponytail. She probably spent three hours in front of the mirror, fixing it.

I turn around and stare at Jane. Then I frown and shake my head, like something's wrong. "Well . . . not as bad as usual."

I don't usually say mean things like that. Jane's face crumples and all of a sudden, she looks like she's going to cry. She's very emotional these days. Maybe she's not preening, after all. Maybe she really wants to know. Sometimes she's very sensitive, like Mom.

"I'm kidding," I say. "You look fine."

Her face brightens. She gets out of the car and slams the door shut. That's what I mean about Jane's being moody about every little thing these days. It must be nice to be a twelve-year-old kid, and not have to worry about so many important things like college and grades. All you have to do is think about your hair and boys and movie stars.

Dad pulls away from the curb, and I settle back into the seat. The radio's playing a soft, low tune. There's a saxophone in it, I think. When it moves into higher notes, it almost sounds like someone's crying.

"Mom seemed kind of upset this morning," I say.

Dad shakes his head and drums his fingers on the steering wheel. "It's that damned appointment. It's routine—I wish she'd remember that. They're just checking on her progress. But your mother worries too much. You know that."

I know that. Of course I know that. We all know that. That's the way it's always been.

Dad pulls the car into traffic, and I can see the hills and houses passing by on the other side of the river. It's cloudy now, and the hills look softer and a little blurred, like pillows holding up the sky.

The saxophone moans again, and there's something so sad and lonely about it, it almost hurts to hear it. Dad changes the station, punching buttons over and over. He doesn't find anything he likes, so he turns off the radio. Dad's a very impatient person.

We don't say anything more till we pull into the circular drive at the high school. Dad puts the car in Park and pats me on the shoulder. "Mom's going to be just fine," he says. "She goes through all these crises—and then everything turns out to be fine. I wish she'd learn that."

"I know it, Dad. I'm not worried."

I reach over and press his hair down. If somebody doesn't do that, he'll go around all day looking like he stuck his finger in a light socket. Then I kiss him on the cheek, and he waves goodbye. I wave again while he drives off. I don't usually do things like that. But sometimes I feel so grateful that Dad's the way he is—especially when Mom's feeling bad like this. He's always steady and happy and strong. I know I can depend on him, and he'll always be there for me. Most people say I'm a lot like him, and I hope that's true.

I walk up the sidewalk to the school. It's called Sam Houston High School, and it's the oldest school in the state. Sam Houston didn't die in the Alamo or anything, but at least he used to be the president of Texas when it was a country. I think he was also an alcoholic. There are lots of famous alcoholics in Texas, but they don't usually name schools after them.

Students are standing around everywhere, and some of them wave at me. A few are smoking, even though they're not supposed to. They like to make lots of noise so everybody can see they're smoking. Most of those kids say they hate high school, since it's so childish. I know a few of them, but they aren't good friends or anything.

Before I go in, I stop and lean against the side of the school for just for a minute. Sometimes being around Mom makes me sad. The funny thing is, when she was going through all those rough treatments, she seemed a lot happier than she does now. That doesn't make any sense to me, but it's true. All the time she was going

36

through chemo and radiation, her face looked different. I don't know how to describe it. But she looked brighter and stronger and happier with herself—the way most people do.

We were all proud of the way she went through all her treatments. She was like a ship sailing off into rough seas, Dad said. She showed how strong and determined she can be in a crisis—what she's really made of. I've never been so proud of Mom in my life.

But now she's different. Quieter. She looks nervous and sad a lot of the time. I don't know why. I don't understand it. I just wish I knew the right thing to say to her so she'd feel better.

What is it, though? Why can't I think of the right thing to say? I'm good at things like that. I always have been. Why can't I do it now?

The first bell rings, long and loud, and people start to move toward the front door. I pull my backpack over my shoulder and head in the open door.

☙ ☙ ☙

"Rory had better watch herself," Emma says. "She's going to end up pregnant, if she doesn't." She pokes her fork into a burrito and a few watery beans slip out. "*Yeccch.* I can't believe I pay for this crap. It's even worse than my mom's cooking."

We're in the school cafeteria, sitting at a small table by the windows. It started raining about an hour ago, and the windows are fogged up. Sometimes, off in the distance, you can hear thunder. Just when I think it's stopped, the windows rattle, and the ground shakes, and everyone looks up and laughs.

Rory's sick today. Or at least she's not here. That's why Emma and Beverly are already talking about her. I wish they'd go back to

37

complaining about the food. Maybe I should pretend to get food poisoning or something and they'll forget about Rory. I doubt it, though.

"Did you see what she was wearing yesterday?" Beverly says. "She had on a top that was cut down to her waist, practically. Her boobs were falling out every time she bent over."

Beverly's always making comments about other girls' breasts. Rory says it's because she doesn't have any of her own.

"Who's Rory dating now?" Beverly asks me. She puts her fingers up to put quotation marks around "dating," so we know what she's really asking: *Who's Rory sleeping with now?*

I stare at my sandwich like it's really interesting. It's turkey on whole wheat with a bunch of lettuce and tomatoes squeezed in. The mustard dribbles out every time I take a bite. I hate it when Beverly and Emma ask me about Rory. Sometimes I think we should stop having lunch together. We act like we're all friends, but we're not. There's Beverly and Emma on one side, and Rory's somewhere else, and I feel like a relay runner going between them. When they ask me about each other, I'm always trying to explain things so they'll like each other more. But it doesn't help.

Sometimes I wish we could just stop pretending so much. But I'm as bad as the other three. I'm always pretending, too. Right now, I'm pretending that Beverly's asked a perfectly nice question.

"Joe Wheeler, I think."

I don't look up, but I'm sure Beverly and Emma are exchanging glances. Joe Wheeler's the richest kid in our high school. He's also drop-dead gorgeous. He drives an old silver Porsche his father gave him, and if you see him from a distance and he's wearing his sunglasses, he looks kind of like Brad Pitt. I know for a fact that every girl in the sophomore class would jump off a cliff to go out with Joe Wheeler. Even Beverly and Emma.

"Joe Wheeler?" Beverly repeats, looking cross. "It'll never last. Rory could never keep someone like him."

I shrug. "Maybe she doesn't want to. Rory gets bored easily."

I hate conversations like this. They're awful! Emma and Beverly are saying all kinds of things, and I am, too. But we're not saying what we really want to say—even though we all know what's going on. They want me to trash Rory the same way they're doing—but I won't. I feel good about that. But I don't feel good about the fact that I don't take up for Rory, either. Not the way I should.

As usual, I just try to change the subject. That's the coward's way out. I know that. But I do it anyway.

"What are you all doing this weekend?" I ask. I try to act like I'm very interested in what they're going to tell me.

That's better. It's a neutral topic. Emma and Beverly go to jocks' parties with their boyfriends almost every weekend. I don't know how they can stand them. Everybody just hangs around with the same people they see every day at school, and they get drunk and talk about football and basketball and baseball. If I was around that kind of conversation, I'd drink a lot, too.

I've been to a few of those parties, and they're very weird. The guys talk a lot, and the girls listen to them like they're fascinating and brilliant. It's strange, because Beverly and Emma seem so strong and lively to me. But when they're around their boyfriends, they act different. Even their voices sound higher.

Emma opens her mouth, then she glances at Beverly. Beverly's staring down at her food, and her cheeks are red. Emma looks at me, but she doesn't say anything. She just bites her lip. She always does that when she's thinking about something. Sometimes she even makes her lip bleed.

"Oh—the *usual*," she says after a few seconds. "Jay and I are going to a movie or something."

Beverly doesn't say a word. She's eating quietly, which is strange. Beverly never does anything quietly. And she never, ever, eats anything in the cafeteria without complaining about it. But she's not saying anything today, even though the food is spectacularly bad. It's supposed to be lasagna, and it looks like the kitchen staff just dumped a bottle of moldy ketchup all over a bunch of noodles.

Emma throws her hair back and glances at Beverly again. I would say she looks worried, but Emma never worries about anything. She's one of the most confident people I've ever met. Sometimes, it's pretty annoying.

"Got to go," Beverly says. She wipes her mouth on the napkin and leaves a bright pink streak on it. Then she picks up her tray and heads to the dish-washing window. Emma and I watch her go.

The minute she leaves the room, Emma leans across the table. "My *God*, Liza," she says in a loud whisper. "Haven't you heard what's going on with Beverly?"

"What do you mean?"

Emma almost snorts impatiently. "I mean—*everything* is going wrong in her life. Her parents split up two weeks ago. You didn't hear that from me, though. Nobody's supposed to know about it. She'd *kill* me if she knew I was telling you this."

Emma stretches her arms up over her head and sighs loudly. For just a second, it occurs to me that she might be enjoying this. Emma's a very dramatic person, and she loves telling stories. But Beverly's her best friend. So maybe I'm wrong. But I don't think so.

"And now," Emma says, sighing again, "Andrew wants to break up with her. Can you *imagine*?"

"But—why?"

"Why *what*?" Emma shakes her head like I'm retarded or something. Her black hair flies all over the place, like it's impatient with me, too. "Her father wanted more space. You know what *that* means." She raises her eyebrows and gives me a significant look.

I nod. Of course I know what that means. I wish Emma would stop acting like I'm the village idiot. Since when did she get so sophisticated and know-it-all—just because she knows a little gossip? Besides, I'm the one who writes the advice column. Not her.

"And *Andrew*." Emma shrugs. "Well . . . I don't know. They've been going together *forever*. I guess he just got tired of her."

Beverly and Andrew had been dating for four years. They started going together at about the same time that Emma and Jay did. I wonder if that bothers Emma.

For once, she almost reads my mind. We're standing by the trash can, letting our napkins and paper cups fall in, when Emma looks at me. "You know," she says, "if the same thing happened to me, I wouldn't even *blink*."

She flashes me a big, happy grin. I've never seen so many perfect white teeth in my life.

"There are *thousands* of guys out there," she says. "Just waiting for me."

❧ ❧ ❧

Emma and I leave the cafeteria together. When the hall splits into three directions, we wave good-bye, and I walk down the right hall by myself.

I run my hand along the lockers and listen to the metal make soft clinks. Sometimes it's a little confusing to be in high school. I feel like my best friends aren't really my best friends. Maybe they aren't even my friends at all. That would make a great letter to "Dear Deborah." The trouble is, I'd have to answer it myself.

I wonder why I didn't notice there was something wrong with

41

Beverly till today. I guess I'm not good at picking up on things like that, the way Jane and Mom are. One time, Mom told me it was better to be the way I am—instead of being too sensitive, like her. She said it was more comfortable to go through life the way I did, not noticing things and getting hurt as much as she did. I know she was trying to compliment me when she said that. But it didn't feel like a compliment.

I turn the corner and almost run into the new guy in my French class. He's crouching by his locker.

"Hi," he says, looking up at me. "First-period French, remember?" He bangs his locker shut and stands up. "I know you. You're Liza—right?"

"Right." I toss my hair back over my shoulder and smile at him. I always hate it when girls do that. "And you're Richard."

It took Rory exactly five minutes to find that out. Richard McKnight. A junior. Just moved here from Atlanta. Drives a dark green Bronco with a bumper sticker that says *I'm doing my part to piss off the religious reich*. Wears blue a lot, which makes him look even more fantastic. Stares at me in French—well, that's what Rory says, anyway. He's also smart, we can tell. He even corrected Ms. Reynolds in class one day. That was very good news. I never feel very romantic about guys who aren't smart.

Richard and I walk along the hall, talking about school and classes and what he thinks about Austin. He likes it, he says. He leans over to talk to me and puts his hand on my back for just a second. His eyes look like soft brown velvet, and his lips are full and sweet-looking. It's a very, very good thing I'm not the kind of girl who notices what guys look like.

"We should get together sometime," he says when we stop at the journalism room.

"Why?" I ask him. I can't believe I'm saying that. I'm acting like a flirt. But I don't flirt! I'm not like that at all.

"Because I'd like to get to know you better," he says.

❧❧❧ ❧❧❧ ❧❧❧

After that, it's hard for me to concentrate on journalism. This is how people start doing badly in school and flunk out and end up in prison and ruin their lives. They're thinking about something else. Someone else. Whatever. But I'm not that kind of person. I have very good concentration. I sit at my desk and center myself and breathe really deeply, so I can calm down and focus.

When you want to calm down, breathing deeply is very important. It's part of yoga. Lots of the books I read recommend yoga and meditation. I'm thinking about taking them up. But I'm not sure I have enough time to calm down every day.

Right now, I'm doing a very good job of centering myself when Ariel Lowenthal comes in the room and throws a grape-jelly donut at me. That's the way kids are on the newspaper. They're not very spiritual.

"Wake up!" Ariel says. "No sleeping on the job!"

Ariel has stringy hair and rhinestone glasses, and she's always wearing a ragged *New York Times* T-shirt and jeans. She's very skinny and nervous, and most of the time, she paces around the room and drives everybody else crazy. Ariel's going to be a big-city investigative journalist when she grows up, and she goes around looking for scandals everywhere so she can write about them. You know you're on to something big when you start getting threats on your life, Ariel says. She can hardly wait till someone threatens her life.

"Any good letters from our local lunatics?" Ariel says. "Wouldn't

43

it be funny if you told them to jump off a parking garage? Old Sorensen would have a coronary!"

She's always saying things like that to me. Sometimes she hangs around and asks to see the most suicidal letters I've gotten so she can test them for fingerprints and save somebody's life and maybe win a Pulitzer or a Nobel. I would never show Ariel a letter in a million years, but she keeps asking.

"Nothing much." I cover up the letter I'm reading so Ariel can't see it. "Any good scandals going on?" That's the best way to handle Ariel. I finally figured that out. Just ask her about what she loves to talk about.

"This dump," Ariel sighs dramatically, "is a wasteland. Every day, I wake up thinking maybe this is the day I'm going to find the janitor screwing the assistant principal in the broom closet. I pray— I mean this, I *pray*—for a killer tornado that would wipe out the entire freshman class."

Ariel sits down at a desk and puts her feet up on it. Her feet twitch up and down, like she's still pacing. She has on black high-top tennis shoes, and she needs to tie the laces on the left one. But she doesn't. She just throws her head back, like she's talking to the ceiling. "But oh, no. I have to write about school board meetings. And boundary changes. Like I even give a rat's ass.

"If I have to go to one more goddamn school board meeting, I'm going to collapse and froth at the mouth and twitch my way up the aisles. It's not going to be pretty, I warn you, Liza. I didn't go into journalism to die from boredom."

Ariel's a little excitable when she gets to talking about stuff like this. Mr. Sorensen lives in fear she's going to find a terrible sex or drug scandal and try to write about it. He keeps pushing her to investigate the pet shelter again, even though we've already run about three hundred stories on it. Mr. Sorensen is an animal-rights

44

activist. I'm pretty sure we're the only student newspaper in the country that's written editorials about not wearing fur three times this year.

But Ariel never listens to Mr. Sorensen. She says she's only interested in human tragedies, and the only way she'll ever do another animal story is if it involves people and animals having sex. "Like some kind of weird love triangle, and somebody killed a German shepherd named Biff in the heat of the moment," she said once. "None of this Humane Society shit."

Ariel can be mean—but she makes me laugh, too. I can't help it. She's mean and she's kind of crazy, but she's also one of the most hilarious people I've ever met in my life. I think she should become a stand-up comedian instead of an investigative journalist. But she says no. She's too sensitive to do stand-up. Which is funny, because I'm pretty sure Ariel is the least sensitive person I've ever met in my life.

After that, Mr. Sorensen comes in the room, and Ariel doesn't talk as much. She offers him the grape-jelly donut she threw at me and picked up off the floor. "It's a special kind of vegetarian fruit donut, Mr. Sorensen," she says. "I bought it just for you."

"Why, thank you, Ariel," Mr. Sorensen says. "Aren't you thoughtful."

He doesn't even look at the donut. He just starts eating it. I hope there aren't any hairs or carpet fuzz stuck to it. That would be revolting.

"Thank you, Ariel," Mr. Sorensen's saying again. He's already finished the donut and he's wiping off his hands with a napkin. "That was delicious."

If you want my honest opinion, I think Mr. Sorensen needs to start exercising and stop eating junk food all the time. Someone told me he used to be thin when he was younger. But now, he looks like a chubby teddy bear with curly brown hair and a little mustache and wire-rimmed glasses. He's cute in a tubby kind of way. But he needs to take better care of himself. I wonder if he has a girlfriend. He never talks about going out. Sometimes I worry about that. I wonder if he's happy.

"How's the article coming, Liza?" Mr. Sorensen asks, about an hour later.

"It's almost there." I'm working on an article about the school band and how they're finally getting new uniforms after about a century. Unfortunately, the uniforms are the wrong color and they're going to have to send them back. They were supposed to be purple, but they came out orange, for some reason. "At this point, I'd be willing to take any color" is what the band director said. "Who cares what the school colors are? We'll never see new uniforms in my lifetime." He sounded pretty bitter about the whole thing.

I hit the Save button on the computer, then I send it. "Finished. It's in your file, Mr. S." I stretch. I've been concentrating so hard that my neck's sore. "Do you need me to wait?"

He shakes his head. "Uh-uh. I'll look at it tonight. We can talk about it tomorrow morning, Liza."

I load all my books into my backpack and tell Mr. Sorensen good night. There's a bus stop about a block from the high school, and I can catch a five o'clock bus if I hurry. I could walk, I guess, but it's kind of wet and dreary.

I'm standing by the bus stop when Richard drives up. "Need a ride?" he says. "You're getting wet."

❦❦❦ ❦❦❦ ❦❦❦

I can tell that Richard's had a lot more experience driving than I've had, because he doesn't get excited and run into things. He can even drive with the radio on and talk to me, all at the same time. That takes a lot of coordination.

I'm sitting at kind of an angle, with my feet under me, so I can talk to him. Well, sort of. I'm also watching him while he shifts the gears. I've never driven a stick shift. I try to see how it works. Richard has his shirtsleeves rolled up to just under his elbows. He has dark hair on his arms, but not too much. His arms and hands look strong. I wonder if he lifts weights. I bet he does. He seems like he's in very good shape. He's wearing a silver ring on his left hand. I try to get a better look at it, but it's hard to see from where I'm sitting.

We sit at a stoplight for a few minutes, and Richard turns his head toward me. Ahead of us, the traffic is drifting by, spraying water behind it. The clouds are low and gray, and the rain sweeps across the streets. I feel warm and dry and comfortable, being inside. I feel good.

"I drove around the school for an hour," he says. He has a very nice smile. His face crinkles when he smiles, and his eyes get softer. They look like they're going to melt. "I was hoping I'd see you."

Driving around the school for an hour? He must be really lonely. Sometimes, I get letters from kids who are new at our school. They say it's hard to make friends, since our school's so big and everyone's in so much of a hurry. Some of them sound depressed. But Richard doesn't. He just sounds—what? Nice.

His voice is very low. Listening to it is kind of like hearing the bass play when you go to concerts. It makes everything vibrate. My stomach starts to vibrate every time he talks. I know I sound like some kind of ditsy teenybopper saying that. But that's not the way I am at all.

I smile at Richard. The minute I do it, I can tell it's different from the way I usually smile. It's bigger, I guess. Also, I'm staring straight into his eyes, and I keep on smiling for a long time. I don't ever do things like this, especially when I don't know someone very well. I think it's a good idea to be friendly to new kids, and I'm

47

always trying to do things like that. But I've never been this friendly before. Sometimes, people get the wrong idea when you're too friendly. It can be a big mistake.

It's raining even harder when we pull in front of my house. I turn to thank Richard for the ride. For just a minute before I open the door, he and I stare at each other.

For just a minute—but it seems longer than that. Our eyes pull together, and it's hard for me to move. There's something about Richard that's different. He seems so sweet and warm and sad, all at the same time. There's something in his face that I can't quite describe. Something—what? Trusting? Yearning? I don't know what it is. But I know it makes me want to reach out and touch his face, even though I hardly know him.

"See you tomorrow," I say. I slam the door and run up the walk as fast as I can, so I won't get wet.

❧ ❧ ❧

"Will you be back in school tomorrow?" I ask Rory. She called the minute I came into the house.

"Why? Did I miss anything interesting?" she asks. "I don't count schoolwork as interesting, by the way."

"You missed lunch with Beverly and Emma."

"I'm still waiting for the interesting part. I think it's time for us to make some new friends, Liza. I'm tired of those two losers. They act like they've got sharpened pencils stuck up their butts. I've had just about all I can take of them."

And they've had just about all they can take of you, I think. I wonder if Rory knows that. Of course she does. She's very smart about other people's feelings. She should probably be writing an advice column instead of me. Except she'd give pretty bad advice. *Why not screw*

48

that guy if you're really in love with him? Go ahead and blow off school.
It's not that big a deal. What do you care what other people say about you?
It doesn't make a damn bit of difference.

Rory's always saying things like that. She doesn't give a damn
about anything. Ariel said one time that Rory was the only true
nihilist she'd ever met in her life. *Nihilist* is a philosophical term. It
means someone who doesn't believe in anything. I know, because I
went home and looked it up. I always look up words I don't know.
They might be on the SAT.

"Beverly's parents just broke up," I tell her. "And Andrew's
tired of her."

I pause, but Rory doesn't say anything.

"So it's a very hard time for her," I add.

"Big deal. That still doesn't explain her sniveling, asinine personality. You didn't see me acting that bad when my parents split
up—did you?"

"Well—no."

What else could I say? Rory's right. Her parents broke up five
years ago, and she never said much about it. Her dad moved somewhere far away, like Seattle. He used to call her and write letters, but
then he stopped. Rory says he has a new life now. *A new life.* It's funny
when people say things like that. When they say they have a new life,
then you know you're never supposed to ask about their old one.

"Besides," Rory says, "you can cut out this sympathy bit, Liza. I
won't feel sorry for Beverly till she ends up with some pimp like
Jonah for a stepfather."

There's a noise in the background on Rory's end. She must be
holding her hand over the phone, because everything's muffled for a
few seconds. Then she comes back on the line. "I've got to go." She
doesn't sound as lively as she usually does. Maybe she really was sick
today, after all. I forgot to ask her about that. Usually, when she

misses school, it's because she's bored and she wants to stay at home and read and watch soap operas and smoke.

I hang up. I never know what to say when Rory talks about Jonah. One time, when we were talking on the phone about a year ago, I asked her what was so bad about him. I mean, I know he needed a lot better personal hygiene, and he wasn't very friendly or anything. The truth is, he *looked* pretty mean and unfriendly. But I'd never seen him *act* that way.

"He doesn't seem that bad"—that's what I'd said to Rory then. I was trying to be nice and make her feel better about Jonah. But she didn't take it like that. She acted like I'd kicked her in the face or spit on her or something.

"That's right, Liza," she said. Her voice was shaking, she was so angry. "You just go on believing that optimistic bullshit you like to hand out to the rest of us fools. Fuck you."

Then she hung up on me. She'd never done that before. I tried to call her back again and again, but she wouldn't answer the phone.

For the next three days, Rory wouldn't talk to me—and it made me feel terrible. I tried to apologize, but she wouldn't even look at me. Besides, I didn't know what I was apologizing for. What had I done, anyway?

But after that, she started talking to me again. Just like that. We didn't say anything about Jonah or what I'd said or how she'd hung up on me. It was one of those things we never talked about, ever. Now, every time Rory mentions Jonah, I never say much. I just agree with her.

Rory and I hardly ever have fights, even though we're very different from each other. Lots of times, she teases me. But it's a nice, friendly kind of teasing.

One time, she said she thought I'd spent too much of my childhood reading *The Little Engine That Could,* and I'd taken it too seri-

50

ously. "All that I-think-I-can bullshit," she said. "Didn't you ever read the sequel to that book, Liza? It's called *Train Wreck*. The Little Engine got to the top of the hill, but he didn't have any brakes." For a few seconds, I thought Rory was serious. But then she started laughing so hard she had to run to the bathroom. When she got back, I pretended I always knew it was a joke.

I press the phone button down for a few seconds. Then I let it up and listen to the dial tone. It's beeping, so someone must have called and left a message on the voice mail. I call the voice-mail number and hear Dad's voice. He sounds upbeat, the way he always does. But there's something odd about his voice, too.

He says that the doctor's taking longer with Mom than they thought. Jane and I should go ahead and order a pizza and get our homework done. I need to make sure Jane works on her Texas history project.

"Don't worry, though," he says. "Everything's fine. We'll be home soon." There's a click on the line, and I stand there with the phone in my hand for a few seconds. I feel funny for some reason—almost like I'm not warm enough.

"Where's Mom and Dad?" Jane asks. She's sitting at the kitchen counter, eating double Oreos and drinking a glass of milk. She has chocolate crumbs smeared all around her mouth. Her face is so dirty, she looks even younger than usual—like a little kid.

"They'll be back soon. Guess what? We get to order pizza tonight."

I know what it is. They don't have to tell me. All I have to do is stare into that surgeon's face—Dr. Gundersson, that's his name—and his cheeks go red and he turns away. He doesn't want to look me in the eye.

So they talk and talk and talk—all of them. Even Will. They talk forever. They talk about statistics and treatments and prognoses. They talk about fighting. That's what I don't understand—all their talk about fighting. They want me to go to war with them.

To them, cancer is some kind of huge, hulking enemy. It's something alien and treacherous they have to fight.

So why can't I see it like that—the way they do? What's wrong with me?

I can't tell them how I really feel, because they'd think I was crazy. When I think about cancer, I see it as a part of my body that's reeled out of control—wild, extravagant cells that multiply and refuse to die. It's a part of me, whether I like it or not.

I can't hate it the way I need to hate it. I know that's stupid and self-defeating. But it's the way I feel. I can't help it.

But I can't tell them that. Ever. I can't tell them how tired I already am after the treatments I've had. I can't tell them anything.

So I listen to them, and they talk and talk and talk. It's easier for all of us that way. We don't have to notice that it's getting darker all around us.

The way it turns out, Mom has some kind of new lump in her right breast. That's where her first tumor was, too.

"I'm not saying it's good news," Dad says, the next morning. He looks tired and his eyes are bloodshot, like he didn't get enough sleep. Even his hair isn't sticking up as much as usual, like it's tired, too. "But if it's malignant—it's localized. *If* it's malignant. It may not be. But if it is, we know they can take care of it—the way they did the first tumor. That's the good news."

Mom didn't come home with him last night. She's staying in

the hospital till they get the results back from the needle biopsy. If the report is bad, she'll go ahead and have surgery later today.

Right now, she's waiting for the pathology report to come back. We all are. "Path reports"—that's what Mom and her group call them. It's strange, when you think about it. A positive path report is bad. A negative one is positive. You shouldn't think positive about pathology reports. A few weeks ago, Rory had to have an STD test, and it was exactly the same. It was good to have a negative report.

"So, Mom's going to have surgery and come home?" Jane asks. She's smearing butter all over her toast. You can hardly see the toast, she's got so much butter on it. "Will she have to do that chemo stuff again—if they find something wrong?"

"Probably," Dad says. He draws in a breath and pats his hair down. Then he smiles at Jane.

Dad has an incredible smile. His eyes light up and his cheeks crinkle, and it makes you feel warmer, just looking at him. It's like sitting in the sun on a cold day. When he smiles, I always feel better, no matter what's happening. It's automatic.

"Your mother did so well on chemo the last time," he's saying. "I'm sure she'd want to do it again—just to make sure all the cancer's gone. It's the smart thing to do. Remember how we talked about how you have to fight cancer?"

Jane's staring down at her toast, but at least she's stopped buttering it. She looks up and her eyes are a bright, watery green. She's crying. "Will Mom go bald again? She doesn't have her wig anymore. She gave it away."

"Then we'll get her a new wig," Dad says. "We'll get her an even prettier wig than she had last time. What do you think about that?"

"I don't like it. I don't want Mom to get sick again." Jane takes a spoon and starts cutting up her toast into little, curved, buttery pieces. She's making a mess all over the table, but Dad doesn't say anything about it.

"Of course you don't like it," Dad says. "Liza and I don't like it, either. And neither does Mom. But after all this is over, she's going to be healthier than she was before." Dad reaches out and touches Jane's hand, and the spoon slips out of it. "It's going to be all right, Janie."

Jane jerks her hand back. "People die from cancer." She sounds angry. Why's she so angry at Dad? It isn't his fault. "They die all the time from cancer. A girl at my school—Suzanne Thatcher—her mother died from breast cancer last year. And that's what Mom has. Breast cancer. She might die from it."

"We're not going to talk about death, because your mother is not going to die," Dad says. "We're not even sure she has cancer again. But if she does, she has a disease that can be treated, and she has wonderful doctors working with her.

"I know this is hard on you, Janie. But there's lots of good news, too—and we can't ignore the good news. Remember, we all have to be strong for Mom. We can't let her see us cry. You know we've talked about that."

Jane nods. She's still staring down at her plate. But she's stopped crying.

Dad looks at me and smiles that same bright, warm smile. He reaches out and messes up my hair. I know what he's trying to tell me, even though he doesn't say anything. He knows he can count on me. He knows I'm strong and I won't get upset, the way Jane is right now.

To tell the truth, Jane cries a lot. She even cries about little things, like when one of her friends gets mad at her. Dad says it's because she's high-strung, like Mom. He and I are different, though. When something like this happens, we're a lot alike. We're very calm in the middle of a crisis. That's what Dad told me last year. We're the kind of people everyone depends on. We're the ones who take care of things.

"Dry your eyes, Jane," Dad says. "We've got to get you girls to school."

It's quiet in the car when we drive to school. Usually, Jane's the one who talks. But this morning, she doesn't say anything. I peek at her in the backseat out of the corner of my eye. She's staring out the window. I don't know what she's looking at.

Jane gets out of the car when we get to her school and says good-bye in a low voice. Then she shuts the door very quietly. Usually, she slams it.

Dad leans back in his seat and sighs. He pats me on the hand again. "Thanks for being a trouper, Liza."

"Sure."

There are lots of questions I want to ask, but I don't think I should say anything right now. Dad's already had such a hard time with Jane, and now he has to go to the hospital to be with Mom. He doesn't need to be answering lots of other questions. He's already told us what's important, anyway. The doctors treated Mom's cancer last spring, and they'll treat it again this time—if they have to. Since Dad's a doctor, he knows about things like this. We'll go on just the way we did a few months ago. After it's over, we'll all be stronger than we ever were before.

Sometimes, I repeat words like that over and over in my mind. At first, maybe, I'm not really convinced. But if I say them again and again, they start to make sense. And eventually, I begin to believe them.

That's how you can live better. You convince yourself to look on the bright side. You choose to be optimistic. You have to do it over and over and over, but finally, it becomes the way you live and you really believe it.

It's not what happens to you. It's how you look at what happens to you. I read that somewhere, didn't I?

❧❧❧ ❧❧❧ ❧❧❧

By the time I get to French, the bell's rung. I hate being late like this. I'm one of these people who's always on time. Ms. Reynolds is already in front of the chalkboard, trying to conjugate an irregular verb. She must have leaned against the board, because she's got chalk marks on the back of her brown dress.

Rory's back. She gives me a big grin while I slip into my seat. She's pointing to the back of the room, so Richard must be there. If Rory paid as much attention to her classes as she did to her romantic life—and everybody else's—she'd be a National Merit Scholar.

"Why don't we move on?" Ms. Reynolds asks. She erases what she's written. She's giving up before she gets to the third-person plural. That's better than she usually does. Sometimes she doesn't even make it to the second-person plural. "I'm sure you've all learned that already—and I don't think it's fair to bog down such a smart class."

She keeps on talking, but I can't hear what she's saying. I try to cover my ears and let my mind go blank. That's supposed to be very good for you. It's called "emptying out your mind," and it's very relaxing and good for your immune system. But you wouldn't believe how hard it is to do—not to think about anything at all. Every time a thought comes into my mind, I try to let it go. I have lots of thoughts, though. Way too many thoughts. That's probably why I'm feeling nervous.

The minute the bell rings, I put my books in my bag and leave the room. I don't want to talk to Rory today. I don't want to talk to Richard, either. I just feel like being alone and quiet for a few minutes. What's wrong with that? That's the problem with this high school. They don't value individual privacy.

I push the girls' rest-room door open and go in. I'm standing at the mirror when Rory walks in.

"You're not supposed to run out of class like that, Liza," she says.

She pulls a cigarette stub with red lipstick marks on the end out of her purse and lights it with a purple lighter. Then she inhales it quickly. You can get suspended for smoking at school. Rory knows that, but she says she doesn't care. The girl next to her waves her arms around to slap away the smoke, like she's choking to death. Rory just ignores her.

"What's wrong with you today?" Rory asks. She drops her cigarette butt on the floor and steps on it.

"Nothing. Nothing at all."

I can hear my own voice saying that. It sounds calm. I always sound calm and I almost always feel calm. That's one of the best things about me, I think.

"Is your mom okay?" Rory's watching my face in the mirror. I wish she'd stop that. But she worries about Mom, and she's always asking me about her. What is it she always says about Mom? That Mom's the only adult she knows who actually listens to her? I think that's it.

"She's in the hospital right now," I say. Rory's still staring at me. I know I need to say more. But what? "It's probably nothing, though."

"God, Liza. I'm so sorry." She puts her hand on my arm and squeezes it. Rory's pretty good about things like this. She doesn't start screaming and scrunching up her face, the way most people do when you talk about cancer. She and Mr. Sorensen are the only people I can ever talk to about Mom. "Are you all right?" she asks.

I nod. I tell her I'm fine.

We leave the rest room and walk through the halls. It's so loud and crowded that we can't talk anymore. For some reason, all that noise and movement and heat makes me feel better. I'm pulled into it, like I'm being absorbed by something that's big and chaotic, but safe. For just a few minutes, I can lose myself there. For just a little while, I can let go.

❧ ❧ ❧

When I get home from school, Granddad is already there. He's going to stay with us while Mom's in the hospital. Since he's a licensed driver, I can drive when he's riding in the front seat. That's a lot better than having Granddad drive. He doesn't like to go any faster than twenty.

He's Dad's father, and he used to be a farmer in the Hill Country, which is west of Austin. When land got more and more expensive in the eighties, he sold his farm and moved into town. The town's called Boerne, and it's pretty, but there's not much to do there. I'm not sure what Granddad does all the time, aside from drinking coffee every day at Mueller's Café and talking to people and watching TV almost twenty-four hours a day.

He looks up and smiles at me when I come in the door. Then he looks back at the TV. He's watching the Weather Channel. "It's forty-five in Amarillo," he says. "Big cold front just came in."

We hug each other. Granddad's bald now, and he wears big glasses with dark rims. I don't know who picked them out for him, but they're way too big for his face. They make his face look like it's

58

shrunk around them. Or maybe Granddad has shrunk, period. I don't know. He used to seem so tall to me. But every time I see him now, he seems smaller and smaller. He also doesn't weigh nearly as much as he used to. Ever since Grandma died and he's had to eat his own cooking, he's lost a lot of weight.

Grandma's been dead for almost ten years, but I don't think Granddad's ever gotten over it. Everything in his house is still the way it was before Grandma died. There are pictures of her everywhere, taken when she was young and had long hair and had won some kind of local beauty contest. I think she was Miss Hill Country Peach or something like that. There's a black-and-white photograph of her and she's smiling and she looks so happy she almost seems to jump out of the picture frame. She's surrounded by a bunch of peaches.

When Grandma and Granddad were young, they looked glamorous together—almost like movie stars. And now she's dead, and when I look at Granddad, I can't even see what he used to be. I used to be able to see that when I looked at him. But now I can't. It's gone. All of it must have gotten lost or something, just like Grandma.

"You're getting taller, Liza," he says. "Better watch out. You don't want to get taller than the boys in your class."

He grins at me. That's what Granddad always asks me about first—boys. He almost never asks about grades or where I want to go to college or what I think about current events, like the president getting impeached. It's very sexist. Dad says Granddad is from the old school and I shouldn't worry about him.

But I do. It's not because Granddad is sexist. I don't think I can do anything about that. He's eighty-two and he's not going to start reading *Ms.* magazine or anything. I worry about him because he seems to be losing his mind, but no one's noticing. His memory is

59

terrible. We have the same conversation over and over, and he never seems to realize it. In five minutes, he'll be telling me what the temperature is in Amarillo again and asking how tall I am.

I guess it didn't bother me that much till Jane pointed it out. The last time Granddad was here, she told Dad it was kind of like having a parrot around who said the same things over and over.

Dad said she was exaggerating. Old people have really bad memories and they're always forgetting things, he said. It's because they've lived so long and learned so much. Granddad was like every other old person he saw every day in his practice. He was a little forgetful, that's all.

For once, I didn't think Dad was right, though. Granddad's memory is getting worse and worse. I wish someone besides Jane would say something about it.

"Granddad—have you talked to Dad yet?"

For a minute, Granddad looks confused. Then he nods his head. "That's right, hon. I forgot all about that. Your mother's fine. Her surgery was a big success, your daddy said." He grabs me by the elbow. "You won't believe all the food and flowers we've been getting, Liza. Come look at all that stuff in the kitchen. We're going to be eating like kings."

Surgery. Mom had surgery. That means her path report was positive. Dad said he'd call me at school and have me paged if that happened. I guess he couldn't get to a phone. Or maybe he was called out on some kind of emergency himself.

I follow Granddad into the kitchen. There are three big bouquets of flowers on the counter. They stretch out and up toward the ceiling, and they're beautiful and bright. They're so gorgeous and colorful, with big bursts of red and white and purple and pink, they make our whole kitchen look different.

Flowers. Everywhere. I've only seen flowers like this once before—when Mom was sick the first time. They're so beautiful and cheerful-looking—so how can they make me feel bad, like I've been kicked in the chest? I always thought flowers were the most fantastic, the most wonderful, miraculous things in the world. And I still do, I guess. But they don't make me happy the way they used to. I don't think I even like flowers anymore.

I shake my head, so I can think more clearly. I have to stop acting like this. I need to get control of myself, I know.

I know what I should do right now. I should take the gift cards out and see who sent the flowers so I can write thank-you notes later. I should also do that with all the food in the refrigerator.

"Four casseroles," Granddad is saying. He opens the refrigerator door and points at the foil-covered dishes. We can't eat all that food in a week. We need to freeze them right now, I know. Otherwise, they'll go to waste and that would be awful. "Which one do you want to have tonight, Liza?"

"Oh, Granddad, I'm not that—"

The doorbell rings and just a few seconds later, the phone rings, too. That's the way it was the last time Mom was sick, too. People were always calling and coming by. I wonder how they hear about things so quickly.

Granddad looks delighted. "There's so much going on here," he says. "Lots of activity. I like that."

❦ ❦ ❦

The phone keeps ringing and people keep stopping by for the rest of the afternoon and evening. Jane and Granddad and I sit at the bar and have some tuna-noodle casserole for dinner. But it's hard to eat. There are too many phone calls and too many knocks at the door.

Everyone wants to know the same thing. *How's Mom doing? How long will she be in the hospital? How are we? What do we need? What can they do to help?*

When they ask those questions, they all look the same, too. They furrow their brows and talk in low, hushed voices and cock their heads to the side.

"Anything you need, Liza," our next-door neighbor, Jacqueline Brimmage says. She's still got on her sweatsuit, so she must have come from the gym. She's frowning and talking in a quiet voice and cocking her head to the side. Just like everybody else. "Anything you need—don't hesitate to call me. All right?"

All right. All right, all right, *all right.* I close the door. I feel like I should lock it and turn off all the lights, the way we always do when we've run out of Halloween candy. I don't want anybody else knocking at our door. I don't want anyone else phoning. Maybe I should take the phone off the hook. I just want to be left alone.

I know that sounds awful. I know that these people care about us and they're just trying to help. I know that. But I can't stand to look at another sad face, and I don't want to answer the same questions. Being around all these people is making *me* feel sad, worse, awful. I want them to leave me alone. I want to feel like a normal person again for a few minutes.

"I've got to study, Granddad. Can you answer the phone?"

"You betcha, hon." Granddad's got a red-checked dish towel in his hand, and he's drying the casserole dish. "I've always enjoyed talking on the phone. Except nobody calls my house much—ever since your grandmother died. She was the big talker in the family. Not me."

He grins at me. He looks so happy that I'm pretty sure he's forgotten why he's here. But maybe that's better. At least he doesn't look as sad as everybody else. At least he's not making me feel worse.

❦ ❦ ❦

I've only been upstairs about three minutes when the phone rings again.

"Liza! It's a boy on the line!" Granddad's screaming up the stairs. "You hear that, hon? A boy!"

"I can hear you, Granddad." The whole world can hear him. He sounds so excited, he's probably going to call the newspaper next.

I pick up the phone. "Hello?"

"Hey, Liza—are you okay?" Richard asks. He doesn't even say hello or who he is. Even though he's from Atlanta and he has a nice drawl, that isn't very southern. Maybe he used to live in New York or something. "I tried to catch up with you all day at school. You looked like you were jogging every time I saw you. What's up?"

I trace my finger around the phone's square numbers. I don't know what to say.

"I just had a busy day. . . ."

"That's why I'd like to see you outside of school. I know it's Thanksgiving this week—but are you going to be in town for the weekend? Maybe we could go out somewhere."

"Maybe we could."

Oh, come on. I'm talking *that* way again, and I can tell my voice is changing. This isn't my usual voice. My usual voice is straightforward and energetic and normal. Right now, I sound like somebody auditioning for a lingerie commercial who's just smoked about five hundred cigarettes. I clear my throat and try to talk like a normal person.

"I can't this week," I say. "Why don't we go to a movie some other time?"

That's better. Much better. I sound like myself again. I'm not the kind of girl who waits around to be asked out. I'm liberated, kind of. What's that song? I am woman, I am powerful. Something like that.

"You're on."

When I hang up, I can hear Dad banging around the kitchen. So I go downstairs. Granddad's in the living room watching TV. "We'll take a look at the Midwest—right after this message," some kind of weatherwoman is saying. She has a voice like Tina Turner's. She sounds like she'd rather be singing instead of reading the weather.

Dad looks up when I walk in the kitchen. "Sorry I didn't talk to you earlier, babe," he says. "Mom's doing great. She had a bilateral mastectomy this morning—both breasts removed. She was awake when I left the hospital. She was kind of groggy, but she wasn't in much pain."

I sit down on one of the bar stools. Dad disappears behind the flowers.

A *bilateral mastectomy.* That's what two of Mom's friends, Jeannette and Barbara, had, too. For just a second, I think about someone cutting off Mom's breasts. She was asleep, of course, so I know it didn't hurt. But what would it be like to wake up without breasts? Would you feel completely different? Would you look completely different?

Mom has average-sized breasts, just like I do. She likes her breasts—that's what she told me one time. She said they were the best part of her figure. A lot better-looking than her legs. And now both her breasts had been cut off. What did they do with them after they cut them off? Did they just throw them away or something? Or did they save them?

Dad must think I have a funny look on my face. "It had to be done, Liza," he says. "We didn't have any choice. When you want to get well, you have to make decisions like that sometimes." He's rinsing off dishes in the sink and loading them into the dishwasher.

"But—how is she? Will she be home for Thanksgiving? Is she going to be all right?"

Dad wipes off his hands with a dish towel. "She'll be here for Thanksgiving—along with all those other people we invited. You and Jane and Granddad and I will have to do all the cooking this year."

He hangs up the towel and kisses me on the cheek. "Mom's fine, babe. Her color was good when I left, and she was in great spirits. She said to tell you and Jane how much she loves you."

Mom's fine. Her breasts are gone. Her color's good. Her tumor's been cut out. She's in good spirits. She's coming home soon. The day after tomorrow, maybe. We have to be strong for her and for each other.

I guess there are more questions I want to ask, but this isn't a good time. Maybe there aren't any good times to ask questions. Jane's just come back into the kitchen, and I think she's been crying again. Her eyes are red and she's blowing her nose.

She sits down at the counter, too. She and Dad and I are all here, in the kitchen, together. But we're hidden by all these flowers, and we can hardly see each other. It's like we're all in different places. All I can smell is the perfume from those flowers, and it's so sweet, it's making me sick to my stomach. I can't think right now. I can hardly even breathe. I can't do anything.

I can ask my questions later, I guess. When I figure out what they are.

"I'm having nightmares, Dad," Jane says. "I keep dreaming about graveyards. Can I stay up for a while? Please? I don't want to dream anymore."

❧❧❧ ❧❧❧ ❧❧❧

The wind's blowing hard and banging the shutters when I wake up in the middle of the night. It's weird to wake up when you've been sleeping so hard. I feel like I've come back from another world.

Jane always remembers her dreams. I never do. Tonight's different, though. I remember everything I just dreamt.

In the dream, I guess I must have been just six or seven, because I was a little taller than Mom's waist. I was crying—the kind of crying you do when you're a little kid. Loud, almost howling. I had tears and snot running down my face, and I'd been crying so hard, I had the hiccups. I haven't cried like that in so long that it's hard to remember what it was like.

Mom pulled me onto her lap, and we sat in the old green rocking chair and moved back and forth. Even though I was too old to be rocked or to sit on Mom's lap, I didn't mind.

"It's all right, Lizzie," she kept whispering to me. That's what my family used to call me when I was a little kid—Lizzie. "It's all right, babe. You'll feel better after you cry."

We rocked back and forth for a long, long time, and gradually, I stopped crying. I even stopped hiccuping. That's when I woke up.

I can remember how Mom used to rock me in that old chair sometimes. I hadn't thought about it in years, though. Everything was so different back then. I was so much smaller and I couldn't take care of myself, and everything was always hurting my feelings. I wasn't nearly as strong as I am now.

Dad was doing his residency, and he didn't spend as much time at home as Mom did. She always seemed so big and powerful to me. I knew I could tell her anything and she would make it all right.

That all seems like a long, long time ago. I can hardly remember it. That was when Mom was at UT. She's brilliant—that's what everybody always said about her. She has a Ph.D in English from Duke and she was teaching creative writing at UT. But she quit five years ago so she could do what she'd always wanted to do—write a novel.

She worked on her novel for two years straight, really hard. I'd come home in the afternoon, and I'd hear the computer keys clicking. Some days, she'd be so excited about her writing that she forgot to eat lunch. She forgot lots of things. But she looked so happy then. We were all happy. I think it was the best time our family's ever had. It was such a good time that it hurts when I remember it. That's why I don't like to think about that time. It's better to just forget.

Mom finished her novel and sent it to a friend who's an editor at a publishing house in New York. I can still remember the day she sent it off, how she kissed the package for good luck before she put it in the mailbox. Then she laughed about how silly that was. That night, she and Dad had a bottle of champagne to celebrate her novel's being finished.

"I think I've finally found what I want to do with my life," she told us. "I've loved writing this novel."

She looked so happy when she said that. Then she and Dad toasted her new career and everything else they could think of. Their faces got pinker and pinker and they laughed so hard, they almost fell off their chairs. It's the only time I've ever seen the two of them drunk.

A few weeks later, the editor sent Mom's book back. She was someone Mom had gone to undergraduate school with, and she wrote a very nice letter about how she appreciated Mom's sending the manuscript to her first. She said she liked parts of the book. But she didn't think it "held together" or "came together" or something like that. Mom didn't have a strong voice—that's what she said. I remember that, because it was so weird. Why was this woman talking about voices when Mom was writing, not talking? That was

67

stupid. I wanted to ask Mom about it. But when I looked at her face, I knew I shouldn't say anything.

After that, she worked on her novel some more. Then she sent it out again, to another old friend who worked in publishing. This time, she didn't talk about it when she sent it off, and she and Dad didn't celebrate and drink champagne. I knew she'd sent it somewhere, because I saw the mail receipt in her study one day. I recognized the name of the woman she was sending it to. We'd met her one time when we were in New York, and she'd told me how much she admired Mom and how smart Mom was. It was nice to hear that from someone who was from New York—someone who had short, businesslike hair and wore black and talked in a fast, loud voice. "Your mother's a very talented woman," she said.

I don't know how many more times Mom sent out the manuscript after that. For a while, we talked about it a little. Jane never did, of course. She was too young. But Dad and I did. Then the weeks passed, and Mom stopped working and she didn't want to talk about her novel. She just sat in her office, and sometimes she read. But she didn't write any longer. And I knew I shouldn't bring it up, because it made her sad just to talk about it.

One day, I came home from school. A cold front had blown in, and it was freezing outside. Mom had a fire in the fireplace. I thought that was great. Fires are really cheerful, and it's hardly ever cold enough to have a fire in Austin. Mom was sitting in front of the fire. She'd been crying, and her face was streaked with red.

"I just burned my novel." She didn't look at me. She just stared at the fire. Then she covered her face and started to cry harder than I'd ever heard her cry. She was almost screaming, she was crying so hard.

"Another publisher sent it back to me yesterday—and I read it again for the first time in months," she said. "And you know what?

They're right. You need a voice to be a writer, and I don't have that. I never have, goddamnit.

"I don't care how nicely they put it or how much they like me. The fact is, my writing's no good. They know it—and now I do, too."

What did she want me to say? I didn't know what she wanted, and I couldn't think of anything. I patted her on the shoulder and tried to put my arm around her, and she cried a long time. Finally, Dad and Jane came home, and Dad took Mom to bed. She was sick for almost a week. She didn't get out of bed for days.

No one ever mentioned Mom's novel or her new career after that happened. Even Jane knew not to mention it. I don't know how—since she never saw Mom burning her novel, the way I did. But Jane's pretty sensitive, even though she's very immature. Also, she and Mom are close, the same way Dad and I are. I guess she understands things about Mom that I don't understand. Or maybe Mom tells her things she doesn't tell me. I don't know.

After that, I don't know what Mom did during the day, but she always looked tired, even though she slept a lot. Sometimes, she'd do volunteer work at one of our schools or she'd tutor some kids in English or writing. But she never seemed happy.

Sometimes, people ask me about how our lives changed after Mom got cancer. I know they've changed some. We had to do a lot more work around the house, and we had to bring her ice water when she was going through chemo, and lots of days, Jane and I had to walk home from school. But it wasn't that big a deal. I felt like we were all doing the same thing together.

It wasn't nearly as big a deal as that afternoon when I came home and Mom was burning her manuscript. After she did that, everything was different. She and I switched places, or something. She was the one who had to be taken care of—not me. She was the one who needed help. She needed my help. I had to be strong for her. I couldn't rely on her any longer. I had to grow up. If I just worked hard enough, and tried and tried and tried, Mom would be happy again. We all would.

Sometimes, when I had too much time to think, I wondered about what had happened that day. *How could Mom give up like that? How could she just let something go and walk away from it?*

I never understood it. I still can't. All I knew was, I never felt the same way about her after she burned her novel. I still loved her. I don't mean that. But I didn't want to *be* like her, the way I used to. I wanted to be someone completely different—anybody. I never wanted to be like Mom. It scared me to death to think I could end up like her.

I know that's a terrible thing to say. It's awful and disgusting, and I'm ashamed of myself for even thinking it. I've never told anybody that, and I never will. Not even Dad. But it's true. After that day, nothing was the same. Everything had changed.

I don't know why I'm dreaming about Mom rocking me in the old rocking chair. That must have happened years ago—or maybe it never really happened. Maybe I just imagined it. It's hard to remember what things were like when she used to take care of me.

Besides, the chair's been gone for years. I think we sold it to someone at a garage sale a few years ago. I came outside and saw a family putting it in the back of their pickup truck. They were all crowding around the chair, loading it in their truck, and they looked so cheerful and happy and excited about it. The next time I looked up, it was gone.

Hours pass, and I don't know it. I drift and fly and float through the air. Every time I open my eyes, someone else is here. Will. The surgeon. The day nurse. The oncologist. The night nurse. A minister who wanted to talk about how much God loved me. Someone from Reach for Recovery, with her tight little smile and bright-colored rubber ball for me to squeeze. "I'm a breast cancer survivor, too," she said. She whispered it, so no one else would hear.

If I press a button, I can feel the painkillers easing into me. I have tubes under my arms to drain fluids and bandages where my breasts used to be.

Bandages. I never look when the surgeon and nurse change my bandages. I prop my chin back and stare at the ceiling and try to drift and fly and float again.

"If you're ready, Liza—we need to start our lesson," Mr. Bridges says. "*If* you're ready. I don't want to rush you or anything."

I'm sitting on one of the couches in the Driving Safe-T office. I didn't even hear Mr. Bridges come in. That's why he's talking this way to me. With "exaggerated courtesy"—that's what you call it. His voice sounds like it's made out of syrup, but his face looks hard. I haven't even started driving and he's already mad at me.

"I'm sorry, Mr. Bridges—I'm just . . ." My voice trails off. I'm just—*what*? Tired? Sad? Crazy? "I'm just having a senior moment." That's what Granddad says sometimes. The trouble is, he has senior hours and days and weeks. "I'm having a senior moment, even though I'm only a sophomore."

So it isn't that great a joke. I know it's not. But I had to say something, didn't I? Aren't you supposed to at least smile when someone cracks a bad joke? I think you should, just to be polite. But Mr. Bridges and Frank don't. They stare at me like I've got some kind of disease or something. Why can't I do anything right when I'm around them? Why is this working out so badly?

71

We drive around town, practicing left turns and right turns. I guess I'm doing all right, because Mr. Bridges doesn't yell at me. He just sits there and talks to Frank. They're talking about football. I'm not very interested in football, so I don't say anything. No, that's not exactly the truth. The truth is, they don't want me in the conversation. It's like some kind of room they've put themselves in and I can't go there.

"All right, Liza. Pull over and let Frank drive," Mr. Bridges says. He doesn't say I'm doing better or worse. He doesn't say anything.

I sit in the backseat and stare out the window. In the background, I can hear Mr. Bridges and Frank talking and laughing. I rest my head against the window.

Mom got home last night. She was dressed the way she usually is, in a sweatshirt and blue jeans, but her clothes looked different on her. She was thinner, and she seemed a little bent over, like she was older than she used to be. I tried not to look at her too closely, though. I didn't want her to think I was looking at her chest.

Jane and I went up and hugged her. We were very careful, the way we hugged her. We didn't want to hurt her.

I helped Dad bring all the flowers in from the car, and we took them upstairs to his and Mom's bedroom. "I want this room to look bright and cheerful," he said. There were seven big bouquets, even bigger and brighter than the ones in the kitchen. Flowers are in every corner of our house, everywhere. It's like they're taking over the whole house.

Mom was already in bed when we got up there. She had a pale-blue nightgown on, and her hands sat on top of the white crocheted bedspread. She still had her plastic hospital bracelet on, and a bandage in the middle of her right arm. Jane was lying on the bed, right beside her. She had her head on Mom's shoulder.

"I'm tired." Mom said that in a low voice, and I didn't know whether she was talking to Dad or me or Jane.

"You get all the rest you need, Bec," Dad said. He sat on the edge of the bed and kissed Mom on the forehead. "We're building your strength back up. The girls and I are here to help you."

I wanted to sit on the bed, too, and hug Mom again. I wanted to whisper in her ear that I loved her and that I knew everything was going to be all right. I wanted to reach out and touch her again, so I could be sure she was really here—because she seemed so far away. I wanted to help her as much as I could. I wanted to do something for her. But I didn't know what to do. So I didn't do anything.

"Good night, Mom," Jane said. "I'm glad you're home. I missed you. It was sad when you weren't here."

Dad kissed Mom again, this time on the cheek. Then he and Jane and I left the room and closed the door quietly. "She's looking so much better than she did yesterday," he said, as we walked down the stairs. "It always takes a few days to bounce back from surgery."

"You planning to spend the night here, Liza?"

I look up. We're back in the Driving Safe-T parking lot, and Mr. Bridges and Frank are standing outside the car, knocking on the window. I wonder how long we've been here. I don't even remember driving back.

I follow them back into the office, walking as quickly and quietly as I can.

Last night, something I couldn't see was chasing me. I ran down streets and alleys, trying to get away. I could hear it and feel it behind me, bearing down. Finally, I reached a dead end and couldn't go any farther. So I turned around. I knew it was something terrible and it was going to hurt me. I tried to scream again and again. But I couldn't make a sound. I knew I had to look at it without screaming.

That's when I woke up—before I could see what it was. My heart was pounding, and my hands were like ice. Everything in the room was dark. I pulled the covers over me, but I couldn't stop shaking. I lay there for hours, trying to tell myself I was safe. I even tried to pray. But I was too scared to go back to sleep.

I've always had nightmares, but these are different. They never go away for long. They wait for me in the dark, like prowlers.

Some nights, my body screams, as if it had its own memories of knives and blood and bright lights. I've been cut open and ripped apart. But somebody forgot to put me back together again.

Dad gets me up by eight, Thanksgiving morning. I don't know why I slept that long. I'd been planning to go jogging before we had breakfast. But now it's too late.

Outside, the leaves have finally started to turn orange and yellow, and some of them have blown off the trees. But the sky is a soft blue, and the temperature must be in the seventies. The windows are open in the kitchen, and a warm breeze floats through. It feels like spring to have the windows open.

"Look at this monster," Dad says, pointing to the turkey. "It's twenty pounds—even bigger than the one we cooked last year. I'll get it ready while you put the dressing together, Liza. I've already got the oven heating up." He's rinsing off the turkey in the sink and pulling out its innards. Mom's the only one in the family who likes things like that—gizzards and livers.

I put a stick of butter in a pan and watch while it melts, yellow

74

and drippy. My hands are cold, so I warm them over the stove. Then I hold the cup of coffee Dad gave me. It's a dark, dark brown. He hardly put any milk in it at all.

At this rate, I'm going to be drinking black coffee by the end of the year. That way, I'll seem a lot more sophisticated. Maybe I'll even be drinking black coffee by the time Richard and I go out. I guess Mom's still asleep right now. Dad says it's good for her. She needs lots of rest after her surgery.

Anyway, it's not that big a deal to make Thanksgiving dinner without her. She hates to cook. In fact, nobody in our family cooks much. Dad says that's why God invented take-out food and frozen dinners. I'm pretty sure the Chinese restaurant a few blocks away would go out of business if we didn't live here. But, for some reason, we've always liked cooking big holiday meals. I guess it's because we only do it a few times a year.

By noon, the kitchen's steaming. Dad's boiling potatoes and peas, and you can smell the turkey in every part of the house. It makes me hungry, even though I just had a big bowl of cereal.

I try to clean up the kitchen and load the dishwasher, so the place won't be such a big mess. Jane finally got up a few minutes ago, but she hasn't been much help at all. In fact, she's just about as much help as Granddad. Right now, they're both watching TV.

I don't know why Dad lets her get away with things like this. That's what happens when you're the youngest kid. You get spoiled. Sometimes, I can hear Jane and Granddad arguing about which station they should watch and who's got the remote control. Granddad's saying they need to check the Weather Channel on the half hour, because that's when they have local updates. We have a wonderful forecast for the whole week—no cold fronts or clouds or anything. But Granddad wants to make sure.

"Why don't you go ahead and get dressed, Liza?" Dad asks. "I've got everything under control."

That's another tradition we have. We always dress up for holiday dinners. It makes everything more fun, for some reason. I guess it's because we're usually a very informal family.

I go upstairs and pull a black knit dress out of my closet. It's simple and pretty, with a neckline that droops a little bit in the front. Mom and I bought it last month when we went shopping. She said I looked gorgeous in it.

We had a good time that day. We walked around the mall and talked. Then we stopped to rest in the food court. Mom and I both got a cappuccino, and we poured lots of sugar in it. I told Mom what was going on at school and how I'm planning to go to a very good college.

For some reason, she smiled when I said that. She reached over and touched me on the hand. "I love you so much, babe," she said. "I'd almost forgotten what it was like to be so young and energetic . . . to believe you can plan everything . . . and mold life the way you want it to be. There's something wonderful about that."

She smiled and squeezed my hand. I didn't know what she meant by that, exactly. But she smiled at me like I understood what she was saying. Mom has a beautiful smile when she's happy. You can almost feel it from across a room.

"You're so much like your father," she said. "So much."

Last month. That was just last month, but it seems longer than that. I pull off my jeans and T-shirt and put the dress on very quickly. I used to like to look at myself when I got undressed because I was in pretty good shape from jogging all the time. It was superficial, but I couldn't help it. I liked the way I looked. Sometimes, I even danced in front of the mirror without any clothes on. That's embarrassing, but it's true.

But now I'm different. I don't want to look at myself without clothes on. I especially don't want to see my breasts. I hate looking at them right now. It doesn't seem right. I don't like my breasts anymore. I wish they would get smaller. But they seem to be growing. Maybe if I get a smaller bra, they won't grow as much.

After I put on my dress and stockings and shoes, I stand in front of the full-length mirror and brush my hair. I guess I'm pretty. That's what people usually say about me. I've got brown eyes and freckles on my cheeks.

I stand there, in front of the mirror, even though I'm not looking at myself any longer. I'm dressed and I look okay, but I don't want to go downstairs. Not yet. I'm not feeling very sociable today. It makes me tired, just thinking about talking to people and smiling and acting like I'm happy.

I lie on my bed and stare at the ceiling. I'm not thinking about anything, really. I'm just staring. I turn on the fan above my bed and watch it whirl.

I wonder what it would be like to be swept up into the fan and shot into a different world and fly into space and just float. What would that be like?—just to float and not feel anything and let go and close my eyes and stop pushing and trying so hard all the time? Right now, that sounds wonderful. Some people can do things like that, I guess. Sometimes I think it must be nice. There must be something peaceful and relaxing about it.

The doorbell rings. It's so loud, it makes me jump.

What's wrong with me, anyway—lying here, daydreaming? That isn't what I'm like. I'm not the kind of person who lets go and floats—and lets things happen to her. I never have been, and I wouldn't want to be. I'm not like that at all. I could never, ever, be like that.

I jump out of bed and put on my shoes. They have two-inch

heels and they make me feel bigger and stronger. Maybe that's what I need right now.

❧ ❧ ❧

Downstairs, the doorbell's still ringing again and again. We're having five people over for Thanksgiving dinner this year. We planned this a long time ago, and we're going ahead with it, Dad said. Even though Mom had surgery this week, we still have a lot to celebrate.

Steve and Rachel Warren are coming with their daughter, Karen. The Warrens are old friends of ours. Sometimes, I feel like we're almost related to each other. Steve and Rachel are both lawyers, but they're nice people and they do lots of pro bono work. They're always taking on death-row appeals that no one else wants and getting involved in them. Karen's a year younger than I am. She's very intellectual.

By the time I go downstairs, the kitchen feels like a sauna. The TV's finally been turned off, and Jane must have turned on the CD player. She loves to put CDs on random arrangement, and that drives me crazy. Sometimes it's playing the Beatles and then it plays Edith Piaf and Gershwin. You can't get used to anything. It's not very calming.

"Can't trust these damned meteorologists," Granddad's saying. If he doesn't trust meteorologists, I wonder why he watches the Weather Channel all the time. "They think they know everything."

"Liza! You look beautiful!" It's Renee Gould, and she kisses me on the cheek. She's tall and homely, with green glasses and hair that frizzes. She looks like a giraffe with a bad permanent. But you can tell she thinks she's gorgeous, for some reason. Three years ago, she got divorced from a pediatrician named Victor, and now she's working as some kind of literacy advocate.

I guess that's what you call a "safe occupation." How can you be against teaching people to read? I can't—except when I'm around Renee for more than thirty seconds. I can't stand her. I know Mom doesn't like her, either, even though she's never said so. She says Renee is the kind of woman who gives the female sex a bad name. She never talks to women when there are men in the room.

Like right now. The minute she greets me, she turns back to Dad. She's standing way too close to him, in my opinion. That's why Jane and I call her "Hot Pants." She practically salivates every time she sees Dad. It's disgusting.

"Good to see you, Liza," Harrison MacDonald says. "Happy Thanksgiving." He's a neighbor, and he doesn't slobber all over me, like Renee, even though we know each other pretty well. He just shakes my hand. I like that a lot better. It makes me feel grown up.

Dad pulls the turkey out of the oven, and everyone applauds. Steve and Rachel must have popped open some champagne, because all the adults are drinking. Even Granddad. That's not a good idea. After about half a drink, Granddad gets strange. His eyes get very shiny and he talks a lot and tells terrible jokes.

"To Thanksgiving—and the good doctor who cooked the bird," Renee says. She raises her glass. Her eyes are as big as a billboard behind her glasses. That's what happens when people drink a lot. She's practically falling-down drunk. Maybe Jane and I should shove her in the oven before it cools off. I can see one of her long, bony legs sticking out of the oven. *Excuse me, cook, but this drumstick is too rare.*

"To Thanksgiving," everyone echoes. We raise our glasses and drink. Then we all smile at each other.

79

"Let's get this show on the road," Dad says. He puts his glass down on the counter and rubs his hands together. "The turkey's getting cold and I've got to carve it. Liza—make sure all the water glasses are filled. Jane—light the candles. Steve, you're in charge of the wine. Rachel—"

There's a noise at the door between the kitchen and dining room. We all look up, and the noise stops. All you can hear is Edith Piaf singing in the background.

Mom's standing there. She's gotten dressed up, like it's a normal Thanksgiving. She's wearing a red fuzzy sweater and a black skirt, and I can tell she's put on some makeup and done something with her hair. She's smiling.

"Happy Thanksgiving, everyone," she says.

For a few seconds, no one says anything. I guess it's because we're so surprised to see her. Then everyone starts to talk at once, kind of loudly, like they're embarrassed and don't know what to say.

Steve and Rachel walk over and hug Mom. They do it carefully, the same way Jane and I did, like Mom could break if you don't watch it. They tell her she looks wonderful. Even Renee runs over and gives Mom a big kiss. She leaves some kind of purple lipstick on Mom's cheek. It's a horrible shade of lipstick, just like what Rory used to wear last year when she was in love with a guy who rode a motorcycle. She always called it "Fuck-Me Mauve."

"You're just in time for dinner, Becca," Dad says. "I was about to call you."

Mom sits down in the dining room, and we bring all the food in. Someone must have set the table while I was upstairs, because it looks beautiful. In the middle of the table, there's a big arrangement of flowers that are gold and brown and orange. Jane lights the candles, and I pour water into the glasses. Even the silver is shiny,

80

and everything looks festive. We all gather around the table and sit down.

"I'd like to propose a toast," Dad says.

We raise our glasses, even though Jane and I just have ice water. Dad smiles at Mom, who's sitting at the opposite end of the table. "To Rebecca—and to her unbelievable mixture of courage and grace. And to her health."

Mom's color looks better in the candlelight. She smiles at all of us. It's a smile that stretches her face in a way that looks like it hurts her. Maybe her face is still sore from surgery. Everything hurts after you've had surgery, she says.

But it's a nice smile, a big smile, and I know that's a good sign. It means Mom is going to be all right and she's getting stronger. I know Dad's been worried about that, even though he hasn't said anything. But now we can all see she's going to be fine.

"To Rebecca," everyone echoes and drinks. The ice water traces a cold path down my throat.

❧ ❧ ❧

I don't like that Renee person at all, if you want to know the truth. The first time Jane and I met her, she almost stepped on us trying to get closer to Dad. I'd just finished watching *The Godfather* and *Godfather Part II* for the fifth time, since they're my favorite movies, and I kept wishing I personally knew somebody in the Mafia who could take her through a toll booth with a lot of machine guns. I know that sounds violent, but Renee's one of those people who makes me think about violent things. I can't help it.

But I don't worry about Renee that much. It's silly to worry about people who don't matter, and she's one of those people. I

81

can tell Dad hardly knows she's in the same room with him. He's nice to her, the way he's nice to everyone. But he just doesn't care that much.

It isn't like the way he is about Mom. I know there's something he feels for her that's stronger than I can understand, because I can see it in his eyes when he looks at her. It's like an invisible current that runs between the two of them and makes everybody else disappear.

People always say my parents are proof that opposites attract. Dad's a real extrovert—talkative and energetic and excited about everything he does. Mom is so different, people say. I can tell that isn't exactly a compliment. Mom's quieter and way too sensitive and she takes everything personally. When she gets depressed, it's hard for her to get out of bed in the mornings.

But that isn't the point I'm trying to make. The point is, my parents have always gotten along better than any other couple I know—even though they're so different. You can feel it when you're around them. They tease each other and they're always hugging and kissing, and there's something so strong between them that I can almost see it. Sometimes it embarrasses me. But it makes me feel good, too. I don't know what makes my parents get along so well. They laugh about things I don't understand, and they exchange glances they think I don't notice. But I do. I always notice, even though I don't understand it.

Sometimes, I think Mom's lucky, because Dad's such a great guy and he's so crazy about her. He's always been there for her to lean on when she gets sad or sick. He's the strong one, the one who can help her, who can talk her out of her bad moods.

But it's never been too clear to me what Dad gets out of Mom, since she isn't nearly as successful or as much fun as he is. I hate to think anything like that, because I love Mom, too. I guess I've heard about so many professional men like Dad leaving their wives and taking up with some trophy bimbo, that sometimes it scares me for Mom. I don't know if she ever thinks about things like that. But she must have—especially when Dad's around women like that Renee person.

I'm glad Dad loves Mom so much—because lots of times, I know that Mom's too dependent on Dad. That makes me nervous. I don't think it's good to be too dependent on anyone. That's how you get hurt really badly. I want Mom to be stronger and work hard and become really successful—so she and Dad can be more like equals.

I don't think a relationship is good when it's so unbalanced. I wish I could tell Mom that, but I can't. I guess she's gotten so used to depending on Dad that she couldn't stop doing it, even if she wanted to.

Maybe that's the way it always is, anyway. Maybe there's always one strong person in a relationship—and the other person is weaker. I guess that makes sense. It makes everything balanced and easier, so you know what to expect.

I hated Thanksgiving dinner. I could hardly eat anything, could hardly talk like a normal human being. In the middle of all that food and music and conversation, I've never felt so alone in my life.

But Thanksgiving was just the beginning. I realize that now. All of a sudden, it's the holiday season. Everywhere I look, I see Christmas decorations and lights, hear Christmas carols on the radio and TV. I can't escape it. But I'm not a part of it.

I know why, I guess. It's because you cross some kind of border once you've been diagnosed with cancer. You can still see the world where you used to live. It's full of healthy people who talk matter-of-factly about the future, about what they'll do for Thanksgiving or Christmas this year—and the next and the next.

But when you're sick, you live somewhere else. It's a world of hospitals and tubes, medical statistics and space-age machinery, floral bouquets and cheerful get-well cards. This world has a future, too, but it's different— shrunken and tattered. You don't talk matter-of-factly about anything.

The truth is, you can't go back to that other, healthy world. You can only pretend to live there, and try to act as if you haven't changed. But you know you don't belong.

That's why it's so hard for healthy people to be around you, I suppose— because they know you're living in a different world. That's why they can't look you in the face, why they're almost afraid to touch you, why their voices change and become more solicitous, as if you're a small child. They don't include you the way they used to. They don't talk to you as much, and they never complain about their daily lives. How can they—to someone who has cancer? "I can't complain. Not to you, of all people." How many times have I heard that?

How many times have I thought, No! Include me. Just for a few minutes, pretend I'm normal. Pretend I'm like the rest of you and I'm still part of that world where I lived so long.

Don't make me feel more alone than I already am.

"My project is about Davy Crockett," Jane says. "Have you ever heard of him, Granddad?"

It's Monday morning, and I'm tired—but Jane isn't. She's telling Dad and Granddad and me about her big Texas history project. I guess she thinks Davy Crockett is some kind of great big secret no one else has ever heard of. These days, she's either crying or hogging the conversation or having nightmares all the time or hanging around Mom, whining. She's extremely moody. I'll be glad when she gets over this puberty thing.

"Sounds familiar," Granddad says. He frowns and looks confused. He used to know everything about the Texas Revolution. But now he can't even remember Davy Crockett.

Jane nods. "He was at the Alamo, Granddad. People always thought he died there—swinging his rifle around, the way he did in the movie. Remember? But maybe he didn't. There's a new book out that says the Mexican army took him hostage and executed him. Don't you think that's interesting?"

Oh, brother. People in Texas start screaming bloody murder when you mess with the Alamo. Dad says that a few years ago, some Arab wanted to buy the Alamo, and the state almost declared war. I can't believe Jane has such a dumb history project.

"That's old news everywhere but the seventh grade," I say.

Dad shoots me a warning look and shakes his head. "I think it's a great topic, Jane. It's nice to work on something that's been in the news and gets people excited." His voice is sharper than usual.

Jane grins at me, like she's won some kind of fight. She's gloating. I hate it when people gloat. "That's what Ms. Williams said, too," Jane says in a loud voice. "She said it was a *highly creative* idea."

Ms. Williams sounds like an idiot to me. She probably told every kid in the entire seventh grade he had a highly creative idea. She must be one of those teachers who's just out of college and tries to boost kids' self-esteem all the time.

I think about saying that to Jane and Granddad, but I know Dad would kill me. We're supposed to be supporting each other even more than we always have. We have to help each other so we can all help Mom.

I know all of that, and I know that Dad's right, as usual. I understand what he's saying. What I don't understand, though, is why I feel so mean right now—especially to Jane. Just looking at her makes me feel so angry, I want to slap her. I'm not usually like this. I'm usually a lot nicer.

"We've got to go," I say. "I don't want to be late."

I'm so happy to get to school that it's ridiculous. But it was such a long, long weekend, and I got tired of being at home. Every time I turned around, someone was at the door or calling. Mom got six more bouquets of flowers and dozens of cookies and three cakes and more dinners than I could count. Every time the mail came, it was mostly full of cards for Mom.

For the past three or four days, it's been very strange. Mom's sleeping a lot. Dad's acting jumpy. Granddad's talking to himself. Jane's babbling and crying, and whenever Mom's awake, Jane follows her around the house like she's about three years old. I'm the only normal person in the whole place, and all I want to do is get out. I'm tired of being surrounded by all this craziness—and all the people who ask me about Mom in sad, hushed tones like they're in church or something.

It's so nice to get to school and walk down the halls. Everybody here treats me like I'm a normal person. They don't know that Mom's sick again—at least not yet. They don't go around acting like they're sorry for me all the time. I'm sick and tired of that. I just want to be left alone and treated like everybody else.

"Good weekend, Liza?" It's Richard. He's wearing a blue shirt again. He looks wonderful in it. It makes his skin look even more tan and his eyes a deeper brown. He should wear blue every day.

"Great. How was your Thanksgiving?"

He shrugs. "It was just Dad and me. We ate out."

"Out? On Thanksgiving?" That sounds awful and depressing, like sleeping in a bus station or something. Thanksgiving's my favorite holiday, and I think you should always spend it at your house with lots of people around. Rory's always saying I've had a sheltered life. Maybe she's right.

Richard and I walk to French together, and I try not to act like a complete moron. But I'm still throwing my hair around a lot more than I normally do. The minute I notice I'm doing something different around Richard, I try to stop it. But then it pops out somewhere else, like some kind of pimple. If I stop throwing my hair around, I'll probably start twitching.

Richard puts his hand on my arm when I sit down at my desk. You wouldn't think that someone's touching you on the arm could be such a big deal. But, with Richard, it feels like a very big deal. I feel like I'm glowing all over and my stomach's jumping up and down. This is ridiculous. I'm acting like a teenager or something.

I turn around and stare Rory in the face. She's dyed her hair a brighter red over the weekend, and she's wearing a shirt that's knotted above her waist. I'm pretty sure that's against school regulations. A big silver locket is hanging between her breasts, bouncing from side to side. This is what Beverly and Emma call one of her "maxima-slut" outfits. They're going to lose their appetites when they see her at lunch. Oh, wonderful. I can hardly wait.

Rory leans across the aisle and taps me on the shoulder with her pencil. "We need to talk, E-*liz*-a-*beth*. We need to talk about men." She grins at me and waves her pencil up and down.

If you're acting different at all, Rory's always sure it's about a boyfriend. Do you know what that's called? "Projection." That means Rory spends all her time thinking about her love life, so she thinks everybody else does, too.

Since we came to high school, Rory's slept with eleven different guys. I know this, because she's told me about every one of them. Eleven is kind of a lot, but I'd never say that to Rory. She already thinks I'm ridiculously old-fashioned because I'm still a virgin at the age of fifteen.

But I'm not old-fashioned. I don't care what Rory says. I've dated a lot of guys, and I've had a good time with all of them. We laughed and talked and went to movies, then we'd usually go parking somewhere. That was exciting and fun—but I just never forgot myself. I can't explain it any better than that. It felt great, but I always knew I had to stop before we were taking off our clothes.

I got excited, but I never stopped being the same person I am. Maybe that sounds weird. But I never got carried away completely. I never lost control of what was going on. Rory says it's because I didn't want to, and maybe she's right. I just know that I'm not ready for sex yet.

I've liked all the guys I've dated, but I've never been in love with them, and I've never spent all my time thinking about them. I have too many other things to think about. I have so many plans about what I want to do with my life. I don't have the time to fall in love with anyone right now. High school's a terrible time to fall in love. You could go bonkers and get pregnant and the next thing you knew, your future would be entirely different. You could ruin your future and get your heart broken, or you could get a really terrible disease and die.

I wish Rory understood that. I'd try to tell her; but she'd never listen to me. I can write an advice column and get people I don't know to listen to me. But I can't talk to my best friend about something this important. I don't think that's good. Like that STD test a couple of weeks ago, for example. Rory was very freaked out. She smoked about six hundred cigarettes, waiting for the results. Everything was fine, though, and now she acts like it never happened. I wish she wouldn't do that. She needs to take better care of herself.

Right now, Rory cocks her head to one side and grins at me. She narrows her eyes and winks. Then she laughs quietly.

"You're dying to tell me about all of this—aren't you?" she says. "You're in love."

❄ ❄ ❄

The rest of the day is boring. When I get to my American history class, Mr. Lambert is gloating about how much trouble the president's in, the same way Jane was gloating this morning. Like I said, I don't like it when anybody gloats. It's annoying.

I stare at my fingernails. When I was younger, I used to bite them all the time, and they looked awful. But I've gotten a lot better since I learned to handle stress. Everybody has lots of stress in their lives, but you have to learn how to control it, that's all. My nails look pretty good right now, even though they're not very long.

I can see Mr. Lambert's lips moving, but I can't hear what he's saying. That's okay. He teaches straight from the book, anyway, when he's not griping about the president. Most of the teachers at Houston High are pretty good. But Mr. Lambert isn't that great, in my opinion.

I've had two teachers here—Mr. Sorensen and Mr. Moffitt—who were wonderful. You could tell they really care about what they're doing—and they love being around students. They're the kind of teachers who make you excited about what you're learning.

Mr. Moffitt was our world history teacher last year. He had black hair and he wore it long, pulled back into a ponytail at the back of his neck, and he was very tan. He was the first Native

American teacher at our school—a Chickasaw from Oklahoma. Lots of times, he'd tell us our textbook was wrong. It was Eurocentric, he said. There wasn't anything in it that was written from the Native Americans' viewpoint.

So Mr. Moffitt would tell us about his ancestors. They once lived in what's now Mississippi, and they farmed there very peacefully and happily. They loved the land and nature, and they honored them in the way they lived.

Then, about 150 years ago, the U.S. government forced them to move to Oklahoma, along with four other tribes. Their journey was called the "Trail of Tears," and half the Indians who went on it died along the way. Mr. Moffitt described it in lots of detail—how sad and brutal it was and how the Chickasaws had to bury their dead and leave them behind as they moved on.

It was a terrible story. By the time he finished telling it, most of the girls were crying. Even the boys had tears in their eyes. That was probably the most fascinating, important class I'd ever been to in my life. Lots of kids said they were going to major in history when they got to college, because of Mr. Moffitt. They said he'd opened their eyes to things they'd never thought about.

A few days later, one of the smartest kids in our class, Ray Atherton, gave a report. Ray's a nice guy, and I like him a lot. He has blond hair that's always slipping down into his eyes, especially when he gets excited about something. That day, his hair kept slipping down into his eyes, over and over.

Ray's report was on the Chickasaws. He'd done a lot of research at the UT library, and he talked for almost half an hour and told us everything he'd found. During all the years the Chickasaws had lived close to whites in the South, they'd tried to assimilate, Ray said. That included all kinds of things—like farming and dressing like the settlers and owning other people. Having slaves, in other words. The whites had betrayed the Chickasaws—but the Chickasaws were still trying to act like the whites, in lots of ways. In the worst ways. Some of the Chickasaws had owned slaves and had brought them along on the Trail of Tears.

At the end of his talk, Ray asked if anybody had any questions. Mr. Moffitt was at the back of the room, with his arms crossed over his chest. His face was almost blank, like he hadn't been paying attention and was thinking about something else.

Sharon Horowitz raised her hand. "Indians owned slaves?" she asked. "The Chickasaws?" She wasn't really talking to Ray. She was asking Mr. Moffitt.

"My ancestors never owned slaves," Mr. Moffitt said. "*Whites* owned slaves. Native Americans did not. Ever."

He walked to the front of the room. His cheeks were flushed a bright red. "Thank you, Ray, for a very provocative presentation." Mr. Moffitt said *provocative* in a strange way, like it wasn't a good thing to be.

For a few seconds, Ray stayed by the podium, holding on to it with both his hands. He looked confused, and his face was pale, like all the blood had drained out of it. "But Mr. Moffitt, I did lots of research on this. There are lots of historical records that show some Indian tribes owned slaves and—"

His voice squeaked then, the way boys' voices do sometimes. We were all so nervous that we laughed.

"There are historical records to show anything," Mr. Moffitt said. "Who do you think wrote history? The white man. For years, history books said that Christopher Columbus discovered America. *Discovered it*—when the native peoples had been here for centuries! If you want to study lies, look at the historical records."

Ray gathered up his books and papers and walked back to his seat. His face looked calm, but his hands were shaking. He didn't say anything.

I can't remember what Mr. Moffitt talked about after that, but it didn't have anything to do with Native Americans or slavery. After the class was over, we were all quiet. We filed out into the hall and got pulled into the crowd. I saw Ray disappear around a corner. He was moving very quickly, almost pushing people out of the way.

What had happened? What? I didn't know. Even though I'd been there the whole time, I wasn't sure.

Mr. Moffitt had been such a wonderful teacher, and he'd made us all so interested in history. For the first time in my life, I'd been thinking about how complicated history was—how we only knew some of the stories. There was so much that had happened that hadn't been written about. How could we be so wrong and ignorant about so many things?

Mr. Moffitt had talked about it all so passionately that he made me want to read and read and read, and look at things with a more open mind and question everything and decide for myself. I think almost everybody in my class felt that way.

And that's exactly what Ray had done. He'd gotten excited along with the rest of us—that's why he'd spent so much time at the UT library, trying to research things that were true and interesting. He wasn't a racist. So why had Mr. Moffitt treated him so badly? Why did he act like Ray had done something terrible and wrong? Weren't we supposed to be looking for the truth, no matter where it led us? That's what Mr. Moffitt had said. He said people didn't like the truth, because it made them uncomfortable. That's why we had to be committed to it, if we were going to pursue it. We had to be sure of what we wanted.

Our history class was never the same after that. We weren't the same and Mr. Moffitt wasn't, either. He gave us lessons that were straight from the book, and even his voice sounded different and lower, like it was tired. Ray used to talk a lot in class—we all did—but after that day, people didn't ask questions or take notes. We just sat there every day for fifty minutes. When I thought about it, it was hard to believe how much I'd loved that class before. I could barely remember the way it used to be.

Mr. Moffitt didn't come back after Christmas. We heard lots of stories about that. Someone said that he'd gotten a much better job in New Mexico. Someone else said he'd been fired. There were even stories about how he'd had a nervous breakdown and had been institutionalized. We had a new teacher named Ms. Strauss and she was fine. But she wasn't like Mr. Moffitt had been. Nobody talked about history outside the classroom, and nobody talked about wanting to be a history major someday.

I hadn't thought about Mr. Moffitt in months, till I heard something about him from Ray this week. Ray's father found out that Mr. Moffitt had been fired for lying on his résumé. He'd never gotten a master's degree in history from the University of Oklahoma, the way he said he had. He didn't have any experience teaching, either. The only thing that was real about him was his name, Ray said. Someone in the administration had called Mr. Moffitt's mother. She lived in Salt Lake City, and she said she hadn't seen her son in years.

"And that wasn't the only thing," Ray said. "His mother said he wasn't an Indian, at all. Not even part Indian. One of his great-grandmothers was Italian though. Isn't that weird? Just like Christopher Columbus. His mother said he'd always identified with American Indians. But she wasn't sure why."

Mr. Moffitt wasn't an Indian? He'd been lying about that? I couldn't believe it. How could he have done that? I looked at Ray's face, and I could tell he didn't believe it himself.

I knew grown-ups didn't always tell the truth. I mean, I'm not that naïve. But would someone lie about something that was so big and important? How could he do that? Why? Sometimes when I think about Mr. Moffitt, I get so confused that I have to stop. When I think about him, I feel bad. That's it. I liked him so much, and now I don't know how to feel about him.

Why couldn't we tell he was lying? Wasn't there something that we should have noticed—and didn't? That's what still bothers me more than anything. How could we have been so wrong about another person? We'd been in Mr. Moffitt's class for months, listening to everything he said. In some ways, his face was as familiar as our own parents'. But we still hadn't known him. We just thought we did.

My girls. I search their faces sometimes, when they're not looking. I try to understand them, try to see what they're feeling.

What is it like for them? What have I done to them by being sick?

They're becoming young women. But just as they're growing breasts and becoming more aware of sex, their mother is diagnosed with breast cancer. How does that make them feel? Like traitors—because they're sexual and healthy and whole and I'm not? Or as if they're doomed? As if we're all doomed, somehow, for being women?

I could ask them, I guess. But I don't want to. There are so many things we simply can't talk about. We have to wait. I don't know what we're waiting for, but we're all looking straight ahead, waiting for something we can't see. Something that will save us.

It's been—what? Almost three weeks since my surgery. My scars are paler now, light red lines across my chest. I'm almost healed, Will says. Almost healed. He always says that twice, as if that makes it more true.

Last night, I felt too weak to eat dinner. I lay on the couch in the family room while Will fixed dinner for the girls and Granddad. It was dark where I was, but the dining room was brightly lit and dazzling. I watched the four of them eat dinner. After a while, I think, they forgot about me.

I felt as if I were in the audience at a play, staring at the characters onstage. They knew their lines and their moves. I was separate, apart from them, invisible in the dark.

I see Richard most days, and he calls me sometimes. But he hasn't asked me out again. Maybe I should ask him out, since I'm liberated. Rory says that acting hard-to-get is Victorian bullshit, and I should take the bull by the horns. Actually, she said to take the bull by the balls. But I don't know. I'll have to think about it some more.

Even though we don't have to finish the school newspaper till Thursday, I stay later than usual most afternoons. There's always a lot of noise in the journalism room, and I like that. Ben Hardy, the sports editor, is sitting at a computer terminal, typing a story. He only types with two fingers, but he's faster than most people who type with ten.

"You remember Doug Ayres—our best football player?" he asks me. "The only decent player on the team?"

I nod. No one goes to football games at our high school, since our team's so lousy. We've had three seasons without winning one game. Not one. The school newspaper keeps track of it, though. Ben says that if we lose four more games, we're going to break the record we set in 1956. That was when the Austin newspaper called our team "a disgrace to Texas public high school football." Ben says any sports record is something to be proud of.

"He's now Doug Ayres—our *ex*-best football player," Ben says. "He just got arrested for grand larceny."

"No!" Ariel says. She lopes across the room and drapes herself over Ben's shoulder so she can read what he's written. "Breaking and entering. Wow! What I wouldn't give to have a teacher doing something like that. Or a principal. That'd be even better. You sports guys get all the good stories."

"Just careful, workmanlike journalism," Ben says. "You should try it sometime, Ariel."

Ariel ignores his remark. "I can hardly wait till Old Lady Thomas sees that story."

So far this year, Ariel's already had one big run-in with Mrs. Thomas, the school principal. Mrs. Thomas censored an article Ariel wanted to write about the percentage of virgins at our high school. Ariel had even come up with a survey she wanted to give people to see how well they understand what sex is. She had a multiple choice definition for oral sex, and one of them was "talking too much while you have intercourse."

Ariel thought that was very funny. Even though Mrs. Thomas censored her article, Ariel still tacked the survey to our bulletin board with a couple of Post-it notes that said, "Way to go, Ariel!" I think Ariel probably wrote them herself. She was the only one who got really excited about the survey. She says that's because the rest of us don't care about the First Amendment like she does.

"Thomas'll be pissing in her pants about this football player," she says. "I think that's great. At least it will get her off my back for a while. You'd think she had enough to do—trying to be principal of this dump. She ought to stay at her stupid desk and leave us alone."

"Fat chance," Ben says.

Mr. Sorensen doesn't say anything. But he's kind of squirming at his desk. I think his theory is that if he just lets Ariel talk and blow off a bunch of steam, then she'll calm down. Maybe that's true.

But every time Ariel blows off steam, it seems to make Mr. Sorensen more nervous. She has that effect on a lot of people.

Ariel goes on talking, which is fine with me. If she's talking about something else, she won't come up and bug me about the letters I'm answering.

I've decided to start working in the journalism office more, instead of doing most of my work at home. Everything seems kind of weird at home these days, and I'm pretty sure I can get a lot more done while I'm in the journalism room. Besides, if I turn my seat around to face the window, I don't have to look at Deborah's portrait. That way, I can concentrate better.

I pull the letters out of the big manila envelope. This week, I've got a note from a girl who's flunking out of school. She's going to die when her parents find out. Her older sister was valedictorian of her class. Someone else wants to know how you get over a broken heart. I think that's from a girl, too. Maybe boys aren't writing letters anymore. Maybe it's only girls who have problems. Maybe Doug Ayres will write me from jail.

Usually, I have fun answering these letters. I feel like I can help people, even when my answers are short. It's important to help people—and it makes me feel like I'm doing something meaningful. That's every bit as important as working in a hospital or a welfare office or an orphanage. At least I think it is.

But I don't feel like that today. I keep staring at these letters. They're all handwritten and kind of crumpled-up, and I keep wondering what it was like for the girls who wrote them. Are they really as unhappy as they seem? Or are they just exaggerating, the way Jane does all the time? Can I do anything to help them—or am I just kidding myself?

What do I know, anyway?

I take a deep breath. I know I've gotten into a very destructive thinking pattern, and I've got to stop. I'm well-balanced. I have lots of common sense. I'm good at helping other people. I'm the kind of person other people can rely on. Of course I can help. Why would anyone bother writing if I couldn't?

Dear SSX, I write. *I know it seems hard right now. But—fortunately!—people don't die from broken hearts.*

❧❧❧ ❧❧❧ ❧❧❧

When I finally look up about an hour later, it's getting dark. Mr. Sorensen's the only one in the journalism room besides me. Sometimes I don't think I have a very good sense of time. I seem to be daydreaming a lot these days and forgetting where I am. That's weird. I've never done that before. I've always been a very focused person.

I'm packing my books into my backpack when Mr. Sorensen looks up. "You've been so quiet this afternoon, Liza," he says. "Are you all right?"

I stuff the last book into the bag and zip it. The bag's bulging now, and it's about to fall apart. I wish someone would figure out how to make a backpack that lasts a whole school year. Mine never lasts more than a semester.

"Of course. I'm fine."

Mr. Sorensen is eating pineapple yogurt, and he scrapes around the bottom of the container with his plastic spoon. That's better than eating pizza and donuts, at least. Maybe he's decided to go on a diet. I hope so.

He must have gotten a haircut over the weekend, because his hair's shorter and a little more rumpled than usual. Mr. Sorensen's one of those people who looks rumpled, no matter what. When he wears a tie, for example, it's always lopsided, and his glasses are usually falling down the bridge of his nose. If he were a woman, you'd say he was "frumpy." I'm not sure what you should call a man who looks like this, though. "Sloppy," I guess. But I don't think he cares.

For a minute, he doesn't say anything. He just pokes around with his spoon. But I feel like I should stand there and wait. You shouldn't walk out on a teacher when he's trying to talk to you.

"How's your family doing these days, Liza?" Mr. Sorensen asks. He's still looking down at the container, like it's important.

He says it very casually. If he were someone else, I'd think it was a normal question. But Mr. Sorensen's kind of a friend of mine, even though he's a teacher. No, that's not true. He's more than kind of a friend. He really *is* a friend. When Mom had breast cancer last spring, he and I would talk about it sometimes. I hated talking about Mom's being sick to anybody, except to him and Rory. Everybody else looked at me in that same sad way, like Mom was already dead or something and they felt really sorry for me because I was practically an orphan.

I hated that. I hate it when people feel sorry for me and act like I need their help. I'm not like that. Not at all. I'm the kind of person who helps other people.

But Mr. Sorensen didn't act like I was some kind of freak who needed his pity. That's because his mother had breast cancer, too, and he knew what it was like. She died from it eight years ago. I knew he didn't want to tell me that, because it might upset me. But it didn't. Not really. So many things have changed in the past eight years, and there are so many good, new ways to fight cancer. It's not even like having the same disease these days, because they can usually treat it. If Mr. Sorensen's mother was diagnosed with breast cancer now, she'd probably live till she was ninety.

Besides, Mr. Sorensen's mother had a bad prognosis from the beginning. He told me that. She had an extremely aggressive kind of breast cancer. Not like the kind Mom has. I'm pretty sure of that. Dad's always said Mom's cancer was highly treatable.

For just a few seconds, I think about telling Mr. Sorensen that Mom's sick again. I guess I could do that. He would understand how it's kind of stressful at my house, and how everybody seems to be going crazy these days. He wouldn't look at me like I was pathetic. I know that.

For just a few seconds, I even open my mouth to tell him. But then I close it. If I talk about Mom, it might upset Mr. Sorensen, and I don't want to do that. It would make him think of his mother and how she died. He was very close to her. I don't want to make him depressed or anything.

When everything's better at home and Mom's in good shape again, I'll tell him what happened—how Mom got sick again and had to go through more chemo. That's it. I can tell him everything later. I won't bother him with it right now.

"My grandfather's visiting and he's kind of losing his mind," I say. "Aside from that, everything's pretty calm at home." I smile at him, so he'll understand that I'm fine. Because I am. I'm doing great. "I've got to run, Mr. S. I've got a bus to catch."

"By all means, Liza," Mr. Sorensen says. He's speaking in a softer voice than usual. Even though I didn't say anything about Mom, he sounds sad.

I slide through the desks and out the door. I can see Deborah's portrait staring at me. Another sad face. I'm tired of sad faces. I want to get away from them when I'm at school. Is that too much to ask?

❀ ❀ ❀

When the bus drops me off, Dad's already home. It's not even six. He must have gotten off early at work.

"Liza!" he says. He's unloading white containers from a big paper bag. "It's Chinese food. Jane and I ordered scallops with ginger sauce—your favorite! And wonton soup."

"And we get to have Coke—as a special treat," Jane says. She's practically addicted to Coke. Last year, she drank fourteen in one day, and she says it's a school record. You wouldn't believe the kinds of things they call records in middle school.

I'm not hungry, but I sit at the bar with them. The wonton soup isn't as good as usual. It's watery and lukewarm. I stir it around with the soup spoon and watch the lettuce bob up and down. Usually, my appetite is much better than this. I'm one of these people who can eat anything.

"Your mother's gone out to a holiday dinner with her support group," Dad says. He wipes his mouth with a napkin. For just a second, his face droops and he looks older. That's weird. He's one of those people who's practically ageless. That's what Rory says about him.

But then he smiles and he looks more like himself. "It's good for Mom to get away—*and* it gives the three of us some time to ourselves. We haven't had enough of that lately."

"Where's Granddad?" I ask.

Dad shrugs, and Jane answers. "He went out to get a hamburger. He said he doesn't like foreign food. I think it has to do with Pearl Harbor or something."

"Pearl Harbor's about Japan, not China," I tell her. "Don't they teach you anything in middle school?"

"Oh, excuse me, you big, fat ox." Jane's voice is blaring, like she's on a loudspeaker. If she keeps talking like this, I'm going to be as deaf as Granddad.

"Enough," Dad says. He puts his hands up above his plate and spreads out his fingers, like he's an umpire telling some runner he's safe. "I don't need the two of you bickering right now. In fact, it's the last thing on earth I need. We have a lot to talk about tonight."

Jane doesn't say anything. She starts eating faster and shoveling food into her mouth, like she's starving to death. She's not even paying attention to Dad. I hope he grounds her.

"Your mother and I went to see her oncologist today," Dad says. "Dr. Mittag." He stops and draws in a big breath. "Dr. Mittag is worried about the aggressiveness of your mother's tumor—you know, how it came back so quickly. So he wants to do everything possible to wipe it out."

Dad is looking right at me. I nod, but Jane doesn't. This is exactly what Dad said the first time Mom had cancer. *Take the most proactive routes medically. Blast it. Cut it out, shrink it, get rid of it. It's a tough disease—so you have to use tough treatments to kill it.* He's not telling us anything we haven't heard before. I guess he thinks we've forgotten. Everything's the same—except for talking about the aggressiveness of the tumor. *Aggressiveness.* Dad's never used that word before.

"Does that mean Mom has to have more chemo?" Jane asks. She's stopped eating, finally.

Dad nods. "Lots more chemo. Mom's going to have a stem-cell transplant. Do you know what that is?"

Jane shakes her head, so Dad starts to explain. He loves to talk about medical treatments. The more he talks, the stronger his voice is. It feels like some kind of powerful wind blowing through here, full of hope and strength and I don't know what else. I'd say faith if he was religious. But he's not.

While Dad talks about stem-cell transplants, I blow on my wonton soup, even though it's not hot. I watch my breath ripple across the top of it. *Hospital stay. Take out stem cells so they can reinject them. That way, you still have an immune system after all that chemo. Give you tremendous amounts of chemo to kill all the cancer cells. A lot more than the usual chemo.*

Some researchers think stem-cell transplants aren't any better than regular chemo. But Dr. Mittag says he's seen patients live for years and years after stem-cells, and thinks studies will show that, eventually. Right now, you have to do everything you can. Everything.

I blow too hard on my soup, and it splashes out of the container.

"Are you listening, Liza?" Dad asks. I nod without looking at him or Jane, and he goes on. "Stem-cell transplants are the most aggressive treatment available for breast cancer. That's why we're going through with it. It's tremendously expensive—and we're fortunate that our insurance will cover it."

"When?" Jane says. She's already started to cry. Tears streak down her face, and she brushes them off with her fist. "When are they going to do this to Mom? How sick is she going to be?"

"Your mother checks into the hospital the day after New Year's," Dad says. "She'll be sick for a while. But she'll have the doctors and nurses there to take care of her."

He pauses. He's waiting for me to say something, I can tell. That's what always happens. Jane gets upset and starts crying, and Dad reassures her. Then I say something that lets him know I'm all right. That makes Jane feel better, too. I'm a good example for her. If I got upset, Jane might have a nervous breakdown. She looks up to me, Dad says.

I spin the earring on my right ear. It's a gold hoop, and I make it go back and forth, back and forth. I want to ask Dad what he meant by *aggressiveness.* I want to know why he's never used the word before—and now he is. What does that mean?

But I can't say that. It wouldn't do any good. We can't afford to waste our time on a bunch of stupid questions. We have to act positively and be proactive. That's what really counts.

"What can Jane and I do for Mom right now, Dad?" I ask.

Dad's face relaxes and he smiles at me. He loves Jane, I know. But he can depend on me. When he looks at me like this, I know how much he counts on me. I can't let him down.

"Why don't you take her shopping for a new wig, Liza? Sometime this week would be perfect. It's time she got a new one."

A stem-cell transplant. "We want the most aggressive treatment if we're going to fight this cancer." That's what Dr. Mittag said. Then he and Will nodded their heads at the same time. "We've got to do this," Will said.

We?

Then they both looked at me. That was a relief. I could have sworn they'd forgotten I was in the room.

I used to like Dr. Mittag. Now I hate him. Him and his stupid, fucking, aggressive treatments, and everything he and Will want from me right now. They looked at me, and I know I was supposed to nod and be brave and strong and go along with them. For a minute, I thought I could do that. But then I just started to cry. Nothing like that has ever happened to me before. All of a sudden, I had tears streaming down my face, and I didn't know where they'd come from. They were noiseless. So was I. I couldn't make a sound. I just sat there and embarrassed both of them by crying.

A stem-cell transplant. How can they talk about something like that so casually? I've read and heard about them—and they scare the bloody hell out of me. You're drugged, incoherent, nauseated, incontinent, blasted with massive amounts of chemo—so much that it almost kills you. It's like going into a deep, dark cave, Libby says, and you have to give in to the shadows,

*let them engulf you and eat you alive. You vomit. Your hair falls out. Even
your fingernails fall off.*

*They almost kill you, then they save your life. The most aggressive
treatment available.*

*"I've been there," Libby said tonight. Our support group was having
dinner together, but no one was eating. "I have been to hell and stayed there.
The doctors . . . everyone else . . . has no idea what they're talking about."*

*Even after two years, she can hardly bear to talk about it. Her face
looks haunted by it, pulled tight.*

*"Some oncologists don't even do stem-cells anymore," Libby said. "Mittag
must think he's Patton."*

"If it saved your life—was it worth it?" Barbara asked her.

If it saved your life. My God. If, if, if.

"I don't know," Libby said.

I'm trying to jog every morning. Dad used to come with me
sometimes, but he's not doing that now. He's too busy with everything that's going on. I miss him. We used to jog along the streets
together, and he'd tell me about some of his patients and about all
the new medical advances that were being made. I love hearing him
talk about science. He always gets so excited and enthusiastic when
he talks about it. It makes both of us run even faster.

I'm slower, going by myself. But I try to push myself harder and
harder. You have to do things like that, even when you don't want to.
The faster and longer I run, the better I'm going to feel. I really like
it when I get completely, totally exhausted. When that happens, I'm
not thinking about anything but running. The only thing I can feel,
really, is how tired I am and how sore my legs are. I have a very high
tolerance for pain, I'm pretty sure. When I've pushed myself that

much, it's all I can think about. There's nothing else left in the world. I like it when that happens. I like it when everything else is gone.

Today, it's barely getting light when I turn onto our street. The streetlights are still on, and there are only a few people who are out. I haven't seen the movie star in days. I read in one of the gossip columns in the newspaper that he's in Rome making another movie, and he won't be back for a few months. That's too bad. I always ran faster and had a lot better posture when I thought I might see him.

A Jeep passes and someone waves at me from inside it. It's Jacqueline Brimmage, our next-door neighbor. She always goes to the gym early in the morning.

I haven't seen her in several days. Last week, she came to our house a bunch of times. "I'm sorry I keep bothering you," she said. "But I've been praying—and I feel that I need to talk to your mother again. I'm afraid her attitude isn't good enough." She smiled at me. She has about six hundred teeth and they're white and straight, like a toothpaste model or an orthodontist's daughter. "You know what they say—your attitude is everything."

She went upstairs to see Mom, but she didn't stay long. After she left, Mom came downstairs. She had bright pink circles on each of her cheeks.

"I have had enough," she told Dad and Jane and me. "I have officially had enough of Jacqueline Brimmage. I don't want her to set foot in this house again."

"Are you okay, Becca?" Dad asked.

"No, I am not okay," Mom said. "How can I be okay when I'm being *stalked* by this optimist? If I see that simpleton in this house again, I'm getting out the steak knives and going after her. She and her simpering, pious little homilies can all go straight to hell."

Mom picked up a pile of the Sunday newspapers and threw them across the room. Two of the sections floated in the air for a minute. "I am goddamn serious," Mom said. "I am not a sideshow-freak cancer patient for these Bible-thumping lunatics to minister to. Do I make myself clear?"

We all said yes, perfectly clear. Mom threw a few more news-papers at the wall and then she marched upstairs again. Dad didn't say anything. He just went upstairs to talk to Mom. I'm glad he did. I'd never seen Mom act like that before. She never throws things or swears. She doesn't have much of a temper, I guess. Nobody does in our family.

But right now, Mom seems different from how she used to be. I don't know what to say to her. I never know how she's going to react to anything, and I never have any idea what kind of mood she's going to be in. Ever since she got home from the hospital, she's been different.

I used to know what to expect from Mom. I mean, she's always been moody and sometimes she gets really depressed. But I knew who she was. She was quiet and a very good listener, and she had a great sense of humor that surprised you, because you never knew when she'd use it. That's what she was like. Even when she was depressed, she was like that—funny and sensitive and smart. She just looked sadder when she was depressed.

But she's not like that any longer. She's different every night. She's so unpredictable these days that I never know what she's going to be like when I see her.

Some nights, when we're all eating dinner together, she talks all the time in a very fast voice. It's like she's trying to tell us every-thing she knows, and she doesn't have enough time to talk about it. She tells us stories about growing up in Muleshoe, which is in the north part of the state, and what her parents were like before they died—when they were much younger. She talks about how the dust blew in the winter and spring, and you could hang clothes out to

107

dry and they came back full of sand and grit. She tells us about teaching college students and about what it was like to be pregnant with us and give birth. Giving birth, she said, was the most wonderful experience of her life.

Mom talks and talks and talks and some nights, no one else can say anything. There's not a spare second for anyone but her to talk. "I can't believe I'm talking so much," she said after dinner one night. "I'm not giving anybody else a chance to speak—am I? I'm sorry."

Dad smiled at her. "Don't be silly, Becca. We want to hear everything you have to say. It's good for you to talk. It'll make you feel better."

Jane and I didn't say anything. We'd both gotten quiet, because we knew we couldn't interrupt Mom and talk about school or anything. I wanted to say something then, but I knew I couldn't. I wanted to ask Mom what she was trying to tell us. What was she getting at? She was talking and talking, but I didn't understand what she wanted us to know. I still don't. Right now, the more she talks, the less I understand her. That doesn't make any sense, does it?

Other nights, Mom is angry at everyone, and some nights, she's sad and quiet. But those aren't the worst nights. The worst nights are when everybody else is talking—Jane and Dad and Granddad and me—and Mom doesn't say much of anything. She doesn't look angry or sad or happy or anything. She smiles this half-smile, and I can tell she's trying to act like she's enjoying herself—but she's not.

I look at her when she's smiling that smile, and sometimes I get this sick feeling in the pit of my stomach. There's something wrong with the way she looks. There's something wrong with the way we're all pretending to be together at that moment, because we're not.

Mom's eyes are looking somewhere else, and I don't know where that is. It's like something big has pulled her away, and just her body is here. At times like that, even when she smiles or talks or laughs, it's like she's gone somewhere else, far away from the rest of us. We're here, but she's not. She's gone someplace we can't go. I don't know where it is, and she never tries to tell us.

❀ ❀ ❀

Richard called last night to ask me out. Finally. I was about to start looking for somebody else, believe me. But he sounded so sweet when he called, I decided I'd forgive him.

Most mornings, after I get to school, I meet him at his locker and we walk to French together. It's not anything we plan or talk about. It just seems to happen every day. When we walk through the halls, Richard keeps his hand at my back. I can feel his fingers on me, no matter what I'm wearing—a sweatshirt or a sweater or a blouse. Sometimes, I lean back just a little so there's more pressure from his hand on me. I hope no one notices that I'm doing that.

Usually, when Richard and I walk into the classroom together, Rory has a big grin on her face. This morning, though, she's staring down at her book and doesn't look up when Richard and I walk into the room. Her hair's falling down in her face, and she has her head propped up on her hand. She's doodling in her book with black ink.

"You okay?" I ask her. She shakes her head and shrugs, but she still doesn't look up at me. Rory's like that sometimes. She's as moody as Jane, even though she should have grown out of it.

Ms. Reynolds passes out our six-week tests. I got a 99. I glance at Rory's test, and all I can see is bright red ink on it. Rory picks up the test and rips it in half very loudly and tosses it up in the air a few inches. By that time, Ms. Reynolds is in the back of the room and she doesn't notice. Ms. Reynolds doesn't like Rory much. Most

109

of her teachers don't. They don't like her attitude. Last year, our algebra teacher told her she was insolent. Rory loves that word, and she said that made her feel proud. She said she wanted it on her gravestone, instead of anything sappy.

That's the thing about Rory. What makes everything worse about her—for the teachers and other kids like Beverly and Emma—is that she's so smart. They'd be a lot happier if she was dumb and dressed badly and slept around and didn't take school seriously. But she's smarter than almost anyone else, and that's what drives them crazy. Also, like I said, she's the kind of person who sees other people pretty clearly. I think that makes other people nervous. The truth is, it makes *me* nervous sometimes—and I'm her best friend. You can't hide anything from Rory.

"Have you ever noticed that life sucks?" she mutters to me when class is over. "I don't mean it's half-bad. I mean it's miserable. I hate my fucking life."

"Is it Joe?" When Rory gets in this kind of mood, it's always about a guy.

"Of course it's Joe," she snorts. "What else would it be? That grade I got on my French test? Get real, Liza."

I follow Rory into the girls' rest room, and we even go into the same stall so she can light a cigarette and take a few puffs. Ever since they've been cracking down on smoking for kids, Rory's been smoking more and more. She says it's her Constitutional right. "Under one of the more obscure amendments," she says.

Rory still smells like smoke when she gets to the cafeteria at lunchtime. She must have stopped by the girls' rest room again.

"Good to see you back at school, Rory," Emma says at lunch. "Glad you could make it *this* week." She takes a huge bite out of her sandwich, and you can hear the lettuce crunch all the way across the table.

Rory raises her eyebrows, but she doesn't say anything. That's what drives Emma and Beverly crazy—when she ignores them. I'm pretty sure they've figured out they're a lot more aware of Rory than she is of them. The truth is, she doesn't care about them and she doesn't care what they think—and that kills them. They hate her, but they think about her a lot.

"I heard a great rumor," Beverly says. She leans across the table to talk to Rory and me. "Lucinda Holt was arrested by the cops Saturday night for giving Harold Rankin a blow job in his car," she whispers. "A blow job! Can you believe that? She's such a slut!"

I don't say anything. I can't think of anything to say, anyway, that would make things better. We all know what Beverly's doing. She doesn't care about Lucinda Holt. In fact, the story might not even be true. She might have made it up. She wants Rory to hear it, though. Rory's the slut she's really talking about.

I wonder what's going on with Beverly these days. Last week, Emma said things were worse. Beverly's dad moved out, and Andrew's dating someone else. I forget who Emma said it was. A freshman, I think.

All I know is, Beverly's face looks different right now. There's something harder and more set about it, even when she smiles. She's always smiled like her mother—dazzling, gorgeous smiles, that were as big as a billboard. *Airline stewardess smiles,* Rory calls them. *Beauty-queen, born-again Christian smiles. A mouthful of saccharin.* Beverly still smiles like that, but it doesn't look right on her face anymore. It's like her face has changed, and she's not sure what to do with it.

It's loud in the cafeteria, but it's completely silent at our table. Out of the corner of my eye, I can see Rory wiping her mouth with her napkin. She does it carefully. Then she wipes her hands and puts her napkin down on her tray. She leans across the table the same way Beverly did.

111

"You know, I don't understand something, Bev," she says in a loud voice. Beverly hates being called Bev, and Rory draws it out in a long syllable, like she doesn't want to let go of it. "What's your problem here—exactly? Is it the fact that Lucinda Holt was dumb enough to get caught by the cops? Or is it that you have a personal problem with blow jobs?"

I've never seen anyone turn as red as Beverly does. Her face looks like a stoplight. I don't know if it's because she's embarrassed or angry or both.

"You little bitch," she says. Her teeth are clamped shut and her eyes are narrow. Even her voice has changed. Usually, Beverly has a sweet, high-pitched voice—like her mother's. This is a different voice, lower and mean. "Just because you've fucked every guy in this high school, you think you can talk like that to me. Do you know what people say about you behind your back—what they call you? My mother doesn't even want me to associate with you. She's afraid I might get a disease—or end up like you."

Rory shrugs. Then she stands up very slowly and picks up her tray. She's a little pale, but she looks calm. "Tell that fat, acne-scarred, Bible-beating, fascist mother of yours she doesn't have anything to worry about," she says. "There's no way you'd ever end up like me. You're way too dumb and you're too goddamn ugly."

All around us, the cafeteria's suddenly gotten quiet. Rory tosses her hair and smiles right at Beverly. "Besides—who'd want to fuck you, anyway, Bev?"

❦ ❦ ❦

After Rory leaves, I sit there for a few minutes with Beverly and Emma. I don't know what to do or say. I just sit there. We all do. Then Beverly and Emma start to talk.

We've all been friends for so many years. I can remember learning to ride bicycles with Beverly and Emma and Rory, and how our front teeth all fell out at the same time. We've still got a picture of the four of us, with our mouths wide open. We're leaning toward the camera, grinning, and we've got our arms around each other.

Every time I run out of patience with Beverly or Emma, I think about that picture. I like having friends who've known me forever. I guess it makes me feel safe—and right now, I'm not feeling as safe as I used to.

But what am I supposed to do? All I know is that I can't go on doing what I'm doing right now. I'm sitting here, listening to Beverly and Emma talk about Rory. I don't look up from my plate, and I don't say anything at all—and they don't talk to me, either.

I keep thinking of what I need to say. How Beverly and Rory are both going through hard times in their lives—that's why they're having all these problems with each other. Beverly's upset because Andrew broke up with her and her dad's living in some apartment on Lake Travis. Her mom's thinking about getting a job, Emma said, and she's never worked before in her life. And Rory—well, I wouldn't tell them about her STD test, of course. But I'd just kind of hint how she'd had some kind of bad health scare, and that was why she was going around saying mean things these days.

I want to say all of that, because it's true. If we all understood more, then couldn't we be nicer to each other? Wouldn't we? I guess not. Because we're never going to be more honest with each other. That's what high school's like. You never, ever, talk about big problems you're having. You always go around, protecting yourself, acting like everything's fine. You always pretend that it's everybody else who has problems—not you. That's what Beverly and Rory are doing right now, and there's nothing I can do or say that would stop them. I might as well quit thinking about it.

"Are you coming, Liza?" Emma says. She and Beverly are standing up. I walk to the trash line with the two of them, but then I turn down the hall by myself. None of us says good-bye.

❧❧❧ ❧❧❧ ❧❧❧

"Thomas has cracked," Ariel says. She's standing in the middle of the journalism office like an evangelist, waving her arms around and talking in a loud voice. "This is a newsbreak. The principal of our fine school is going pathetically, frothing-at-the-mouth nuts. Will someone please call the little men in white suits so they can take her away? It's the only merciful thing to do."

For once, Ariel isn't exaggerating much. She's waving around a memo to students and teachers from Mrs. Thomas. Mrs. Thomas is really concerned about gangs in our school, and yesterday, somebody made an anonymous phone call to her office to report that some gang named the Executioners had targeted our school. The way you know someone's a member of the Executioners, the caller said, is that they wear the color red.

That's what Mrs. Thomas's memo is about. She's banned the color red at Sam Houston High School. Nobody can wear it—not even teachers—"until this grave threat to our school has been surmounted and vanquished," the memo says. When Mrs. Thomas gets excited, she loves to use big words.

"Thank God our school colors aren't red," Ariel's saying melodramatically. "Can you imagine the upheaval? We'd have to kill the whole football team when they suited up. We'd have to massacre them before the other team did."

Mr. Sorensen shakes his head and leans over to read something more carefully. It's a communiqué from an animal-rights group he's

114

a member of. He wants Ariel to write another op-ed piece about cruelty to animals, and Ariel's trying to get out of it.

A professor at UT is doing electrical-shock experiments on rats, and Mr. Sorensen has been upset about it for the past few days. He says he used to be a moderate about animal rights. But now he's been radicalized. He must be really upset, because his face looks white today.

"Think about it, Ariel," he said yesterday. "You could take an entirely new slant on the story. You could write it from the animal's point of view. What's it like to have experimenters work on you for their own gain? It could be a prizewinner. The Humane Society gives lots of awards every year."

Ariel almost yawned in his face when he said that. "I'll certainly give it some thought, Mr. Sorensen," she said. She was peeling the paper off a cupcake and letting the crumbs fall all over his desk. Every time some crumbs fell, Mr. Sorensen would sweep them off and throw them in his wastebasket. But Ariel never noticed.

"Don't you think we've kind of OD'd on all those animal stories this year?" she said. "I think we need to concentrate on raw, stark, devastating human tragedy for a change. I wish I could find one."

Mr. Sorensen just nodded. I think he's given up on recruiting people in journalism to the animal-rights movement. He thinks we're a cynical bunch—that's what he said one time. He was talking in a very sad voice, and it made me feel bad.

I know I'm Mr. Sorensen's favorite student, but I haven't gone to any demonstrations with him or helped him make signs. I feel bad about that, too.

Besides, I'm positive he knows Mom is sick again. I can tell by the way he looks at me and talks to me. Someone must have told him. Even though Austin's grown, it's like a small town sometimes.

People here gossip a lot. Especially about things like cancer. I don't know why they do. It's not anybody else's business. I thought the Constitution was supposed to give us privacy or something like that. I hope nobody else in the school knows. I'd be extremely embarrassed if that happened. Like I said, it's nobody's business. Nobody's.

I think Mr. Sorensen doesn't want to bring up the whole subject. He's waiting for me to tell him about Mom. And I want to talk to him, I guess. But I don't know what I'd say. Mom's sick and she's going to have a stem-cell transplant and she's acting stranger than I've ever seen her act before. Jane's crying and having nightmares all the time. Dad's a nervous wreck. Granddad's losing his mind. How could I ever say anything like that? I couldn't. I can't talk about my family that way. It wouldn't be right.

That's why I've been avoiding Mr. Sorensen. I don't want him to have the chance to ask how everything is with me. He wouldn't understand, even if I told him what was happening. No one would understand. If I don't know what's going on, and I'm part of the family—how could anyone else?

It wouldn't help to talk about it. I can't talk about it. It would just make everything worse. I don't even want to think about it—and I wish I could stop. But I can't, for some reason. It just keeps swirling around in my mind, faster and faster. I want to stop it, but I can't.

Ariel clears her throat, and I jump about a foot into the air. She's standing right behind me. I wonder how long she's been there.

"That was certainly an entertaining spectacle at your lunch table today, Liza," she says. "You and your friends are usually so well-behaved, too. I thought Beverly Proctor was going to shit in her pants. Too bad somebody didn't have a camera."

"Mmmmmm." I try to look even more intently at the computer screen. The truth is, I don't have much work to do. But I want to be here, where everyone's talking and laughing and shooting paper wads into the wastebaskets. It makes me feel better. I don't want to go home. I stare at the computer screen like it's the most fascinating thing I've ever seen in my life.

The last thing I want to do is talk to Ariel about what happened at lunch. I put my head down and pretend to be very, very busy.

Finally, Ariel leaves me alone and wanders off to another computer. Unfortunately, she's chewing bubble gum, and she sits at the terminal, popping it like a bunch of firecrackers. Out of the corner of my eye, I can see her blowing big purple bubbles that finally break all over her face. Someone should tell her that gum is bad for your teeth, unless you get the sugar-free kind.

I keep on acting like I'm working. I check my e-mail and send a note to my cousin Eleanor in Dallas. She wants to know how Mom's doing. I tell her Mom's fine. The surgery went beautifully, and she's going to be starting treatments in January. I don't say anything more about the treatment. It's kind of complicated to get into on e-mail. So I tell Eleanor that Dad and Jane and I are fine, too, but Jane's going through a difficult adolescence and cries too much. Eleanor has a younger sister, too, so I'm sure she'll understand.

I stretch my neck from one side to the other. Mr. Sorensen still looks pale. I wonder if anything's wrong with him. The next time I look up, he's standing by his desk, pulling his jacket on. It's a gray nylon jacket that looks like it's about a million years old, with lots of strings dangling from it. I hate to see him in that jacket. It always makes him look lonely and sad. I think a new jacket would make him feel a lot better. I wish he'd get one soon.

"Kids," he says. "I don't feel well. I need to go home now." He pulls the jacket hood up over his hair, even though he's still in the classroom, and tightens it around his face. It looks terrible on him. Next to the hood, his face looks gray, too. All you can really see are

117

his glasses slipping down his nose. He pushes them up with his finger. "I think I've proofed everything, haven't I? It's a good thing we're early this week."

Ariel raises her hand lazily into the air. "I'm still working on my op-ed piece, Mr. Sorensen. It's about Mrs. Thomas's edict against wearing red. I think we need some kind of coverage of that, don't you?"

Mr. Sorensen nods. I think he's relieved Ariel's writing about something like that, instead of her usual sex-and-drugs-and-murder obsessions. "How much longer will it be, Ariel?"

Ariel shrugs and sighs. "At least an hour, Mr. S. You know what a slow writer I am. I don't want to keep you if you're feeling bad. Can we get somebody else to look at it so you can go?"

"I'll look at it, Mr. Sorensen," I say. Why not? I'm not doing that much, anyway, and I'm not in a big hurry to get home.

"Great. Thank you, Liza."

Mr. Sorensen picks up his books and heads out the door. There are only three of us left in the room—me, Ariel, and Ben. That's what a newspaper's like. It's really crowded and crazy up till the deadline, which was supposed to be yesterday. But Mr. Sorensen says we can always have a little more time, if we need it, for important articles. I wish I still had something to work on, but I don't. The whole place is like a tomb. Right now is a good time to concentrate, since it's so quiet and empty. But there's nothing left to concentrate on. I wish I had something important to think about.

I answer more e-mail and write friends I haven't heard from in weeks. Half an hour later, I wander out into the hall and get a drink of water at the fountain. Richard's standing there. I get a little wobbly, just looking at him. I can't help it. I wish I'd get over this, but it just seems to be getting worse. Maybe there's some kind of drug I could take that would calm me down.

"I didn't think you'd ever come out," he says. "You need a ride home?"

He follows me back into the journalism room, and I gather up my jacket and backpack and switch off the computer. Nobody else is in the office, so I switch off the light and close the door. I can hear it lock behind me.

We don't talk that much while Richard drives me home. It gets dark early now, and the streets are full of cars with their headlights on, moving in and out of the lanes. Richard drives wonderfully. Not too fast, not too slow. Very smoothly, the way you're supposed to. I'm glad I'm not driving. I think I need to drop out of driver's ed. Every time I'm in the car with Frank and Mr. Bridges, I can't concentrate. It's like every time I drive, I'm getting worse, instead of better.

Yesterday, when I was driving with them, I almost ran a red light. "What in the hell do you think you're doing, Liza?" Mr. Bridges said. Well, he didn't exactly say it. He was shouting at me.

After that, I kept trying to talk to myself about learning from my mistakes and going on. But it was hard. Frank was laughing in the backseat, and I couldn't think about anything the way I needed to. I wanted to pull the car over to the curb and cry for a long time because I was so embarrassed. But I wouldn't do that for a million dollars. I never cry in front of other people—especially in front of people like that.

Besides, I can't drop out of driver's ed. Dad's already talking about how great it is that I'm going to be sixteen in January—and what a big help it will be for me to have my license when Mom's not feeling well. He says the timing is perfect. I can't tell him what's going on in driver's ed, anyway. It's something I've got to handle by myself. Dad has enough going on right now.

Richard brakes the car to a stop, right in front of our house. He also brakes very smoothly. That's something I need to work on, too.

I turn toward him. He's looking right at me, and his eyes are beautiful and soft and warm. There's so much—I don't know, tenderness—in the way he's looking at me. I've never had anybody look at me this way before, like they really need me. That's it. That's the difference.

I shut my eyes. I can feel his arms around my shoulders and his lips touching my face and then my mouth. I push up against him and stroke his cheek softly with my hand. Everywhere he's touching me and kissing me, I feel warm. I feel warm and alive and wonderful—but I feel something else, too. I feel safe. I used to feel safe all the time. But now I don't. Not the way I used to.

I have to go, I keep telling myself. I have to go. We haven't even had a date yet. Not a real one. I don't know him that well. What am I doing? I've got to stop this. But I don't want to. I want it to go on and on and on. It feels wonderful.

Finally, I pull myself away from him and slide across the seat, back to my side. I try to pat my hair. It's a mess. Also, my T-shirt is twisted around. I feel like I've been on one of those dangerous rides at the amusement park where you're whirling and spinning around and getting thrown all over the place.

We sit, facing each other. For a few seconds, we don't say anything. We're both breathing hard, I notice.

"We're going out Saturday night," he says. "Remember?"

Remember? Is he kidding? "Of course I do," I say.

❧ ❧ ❧

Dad and Granddad and Jane are cooking dinner when I walk in the house. Well, *cooking* is kind of an exaggeration. They're heating up one of the frozen casseroles somebody brought us while Mom was in the hospital.

120

Dad's even got on an apron that's wrapped around his middle a couple of times. He looks thinner than usual, and a lot more tired. Even his eyes don't look as bright and lively as they usually do. He kisses me on the cheek, but I can tell he doesn't really notice what he's doing. He gets like this sometimes. He calls it "being on automatic."

I'm glad they're all busy, though. I don't want them to look at me too closely. I'm pretty sure I must look different, and I don't want them to notice. Also, I don't want to talk much. I have too many other things to think about. Like Richard.

"Oh, no! This casserole has meat," Jane says, like *meat* is the dirtiest word she's ever heard in her life. "I can't eat meat. I'm a vegetarian."

"A what?" Granddad asks.

"A vegetarian, Granddad. That means I don't eat meat."

Granddad nods. He gets lots of right-wing propaganda in the mail, so I bet he's heard of vegetarians before. They're usually mentioned in the same sentences as bleeding-heart liberals and communists and drug addicts and hippies. I bet he's already decided Jane's a communist. He doesn't know she's only been a vegetarian since the day after Thanksgiving—three weeks ago. She pigged out on turkey the whole day and now, all she can talk about is how she's a vegetarian. What a joke. She's doing this just to get attention.

"Don't worry," Jane says loudly. "I've got my own tofu in the refrigerator."

I set the table and we sit down. Granddad's sitting where Mom usually sits, at the end of the table opposite Dad. "Your mother's not hungry tonight" is what Dad says. He says it in a funny way that means he doesn't want us to ask him about it. But naturally, Jane doesn't get the hint.

"Is Mom okay?" Her voice is higher than usual.

Dad's staring at some place on the wall, chewing. "She had a bad day today, that's all. All of us have bad days sometimes, Janie. It's perfectly normal."

"What's wrong with Rebecca?" Granddad asks. "Is she sick or something? She didn't look a-tall well when I saw her this afternoon. Kinda worried me."

That's what I mean about Granddad. He's supposed to be helping us while Mom's sick—but he's already forgotten why he's here. Maybe he's forgotten he doesn't live here full-time.

"She's really sick, Granddad," Jane says. "She has cancer."

She stares at Dad after she says that. She looks angry, the way she did the other day. We almost never mention the word *cancer*, especially not at the dinner table. I feel like Jane's done something rude—like she belched at the table or something. Can't she tell Dad doesn't want to talk about this? Why does she always have to make things worse?

"Rebecca's under a lot of stress," Dad tells Granddad. He looks sad, like he's probably explained this to Granddad about a hundred times already. "She's going into the hospital in a couple of weeks for a stem-cell transplant. She knows it's the best thing for her to do—but she's nervous about it."

I've never seen Dad look this bad. His face looks almost hollow, like his cheeks have sunk in. He must feel like he's the one who has to do everything for us, for our whole family. He's not the kind of person who looks sad and tired like this. He's wrong about saying we all have bad days, because he never does. *He doesn't allow them to happen*—that's what he's always said to me. He never gives in to them. He never gives in, never gives up. Ever.

"Mom always gets nervous when she has to do something new," I say. "But she'll be fine, Granddad." I'm not really speaking to Granddad, though. I know he'll forget what I'm saying the minute the words are out of my mouth. I'm speaking so that Dad and Jane will hear me.

"A girl at my school—her mother died from breast cancer," Jane says. "She *died*."

"You've already told us about that," I say, before Dad can open his mouth. I want to kill Jane. Can't she see she's making everything worse? The words pour out of my mouth, faster and faster. "So what? Mom's not going to die. Why don't you just shut up if you can't say anything good?"

"Why don't *you* just shut up, Liza? You're acting like a dumb bitch." Jane throws her napkin at the plate and leaves the table. She doesn't even ask to be excused. Also, she's not supposed to talk like that. But Dad doesn't say anything to her.

Jane runs upstairs and then her door slams. She's not supposed to do that, either.

Dad and Granddad and I sit at the table, and we try to eat and talk. But we don't say much. When I clear the table, I see that we've all left most of the food on our plates. Jane's tofu is lying there like a bunch of white, wobbly Jell-O.

I stuff it all down the drain and run the disposal. What a waste. I was in the first good mood I've been in in ages. But now Jane's ruined it.

❈ ❈ ❈

"Tell me everything," Rory says. "I want details. Sordid details. We know he's great-looking. But is he a good kisser?"

I should be studying, but Rory called a few minutes ago. I thought she might want to talk about what happened at lunch today. But she hasn't said anything about it. Instead, she's been asking me all about Richard.

"Is he a good kisser?" I echo. "Oh, my God . . . is he a good kisser . . ." My voice trails off. I don't seem to be expressing myself very well today.

"Uh-huh," Rory drawls. "I thought so. You can always tell by the way they walk." She pauses. "Let me guess. You've never been kissed that way before—have you?"

"Of course I have. Lots of times. Remember Tom? I kissed him a million times—and he's a junior. It's not that big a deal. Stop acting like I'm a baby."

"But you've never acted this excited before—have you, Miss Perfect? You're practically panting over the phone. Tell Rory everything, baby. She knows the voice of raw sexual excitement when she hears it."

"I can't talk. Jane's in the next room. She's at a very impressionable age."

I wish Rory would keep asking me about Richard, but she doesn't. She tells me about a book she's been reading, instead of the one we're supposed to read in American literature. It's about a man who can't get out of bed in the mornings. "It's another one of those Russian novels," she says. "They're vastly superior to that crap we read at school."

But I'm barely listening. All I want to do is lean back and think what it felt like when Richard kissed me. Rory's right, but I'm not going to tell her. I've never been kissed that way before. It's like a completely different experience. Maybe that's what people mean when they write me and say it's hard not to go too far with guys they like. I've always thought they just didn't have any self-control. But maybe they were feeling something different from what I was. Maybe this is why people make such a big deal out of sex.

Finally, Rory says she has to get off, and we both hang up. I wander down the hall. The light's on in Mom and Dad's room, and I knock. I hear a voice saying to come in. It's Mom, and her voice is far away. I step in and look. Jane's lying on Mom and Dad's bed, with her head propped on her hand. She's talking to Mom, I guess. I ignore her. She still owes me an apology for the way she acted at dinner tonight.

Mom's in the master bathroom. She's standing with her back to me, in front of the mirror that stretches all the way across the wall. It has lights on top of it, like a great big makeup mirror.

For just a few seconds, I see what Mom's staring at. Her chest is completely flat. She has two thin, red scars—like two slashes—across her chest.

I've seen lots of scars before. I've got one on my leg, where I had eight stitches after someone kicked me playing soccer. The body mends itself with scars, Dad says. It makes itself even stronger than before. Scars aren't a big deal.

But I've never seen scars like this before. For some reason, they're different, worse, terrible. They're making me sick. I feel like I'm going to faint.

Mom pulls her nightgown over her head, and everything disappears. The scars are all covered up with folds of baby-blue flannel. Everything looks normal again.

"Are you all right, Liza? You look pale, babe." Mom takes my arm, and we walk back into her bedroom. She sits on the bed and pulls me down beside her. Behind us, I can feel Jane squirming on the bed.

Mom puts her arm around me and squeezes my neck. For just a few seconds, I snuggle up next to her and close my eyes. I smell the faint, sweet odor of the perfume she always wears—L'Air du Temps—mixed with her skin. Even though I'm almost grown up, Mom's smell is still the most familiar thing on earth to me, something I've always known.

125

"I'm fine," I tell her.

There are so many other things I want to say, so many other things I need to say. But I can't act like a baby—the way Jane is. I know Mom's been feeling worse, and I need to help cheer her up. She needs everybody around her to be more positive and help her through this. She needs me to be strong, and I'm hardly saying anything. Instead, she's the one who's talking to me, trying to help me. That isn't right.

"I know it's hard to see—well, to see those scars," Mom's saying. Her voice is low and quiet. "At first, I wanted to spare you and Jane that. But now I feel differently about it. I think it may be better to go ahead and look at them—better for all of us."

I can tell she's not sure about what she's saying, though. She probably noticed that I wanted to faint or run away when I saw her. I can't let her think that. Besides, now that I'm sitting down and she's got her nightgown back on, I'm feeling better. I'm going to be fine.

"It's all right. It's really all right, Mom. I was just surprised— that's all."

Mom acts like she doesn't hear me. "Do you know what I mean, babe? I've been thinking about this a lot. It's better to look at things that scare you—instead of running away from them."

"No, really, Mom. I'm all right. I'm not scared of anything."

Mom stares down at her hands and doesn't say anything. For some reason, I have the feeling she's disappointed with me. I feel the same way I do when I look at that portrait of Deborah Ames on the journalism wall. I've done something wrong. I'm letting someone else down and I don't know why. I keep trying and trying, but somehow I know it's not going to matter. I've done something wrong, but I'm not sure what it is, and nobody's going to tell me.

"There . . . there's so much I want to say to both you girls. . . ."

126

Mom's voice is still low and quiet, and she acts like she's not listening to me. "But I don't think you want to hear what I'm saying."

It's silent for a few seconds. I can hear Jane breathing loudly behind us. Then she starts to talk in one of those loud teenager voices she's been using all the time. "I'd like to hear you talk, Mom," she says. "But you spend so much time with your stupid support group—instead of us. Why do you keep doing that?"

Mom smoothes her nightgown down, running her hands up and down the material. Then she turns around so she can talk to Jane and me both. When I see her, I realize it's happening again. Something in her face has changed, like it's closed and empty. She's moved somewhere else, slipped out of the room while we weren't looking.

"It's hard to explain," she says. It's still Mom's voice, but it sounds heavier and sadder. "But they're the only people who understand me right now. They're the only people who are willing to listen . . . to what I really want to say. No one else wants to hear it."

After she stops talking, the room's even quieter. I sit as still as I can, trying not to move. So does Jane. She's so quiet now, I can hardly hear her breathe.

Why do they shut me out and walk away from me? Don't they know how much they're hurting me?

I try to talk, the way I did tonight with Liza and Jane. God, I want so badly for us to be able to talk to each other, for them to hear what I need to tell them. But they don't want to know. It terrifies them when I want to talk about my illness. Their faces go blank, and we lose each other again and again. We're blind and deaf to each other. We're supposed to be a family, aren't we? But we aren't, right now. We're all lost and alone. We can't even comfort each other. We've become strangers.

It's three in the morning, but I'm still awake. I'm lying here beside Will, and he's already asleep. His breaths are long and loud. It used to comfort me to hear him sleep so soundly. I would reach over and touch him, and I'd feel safe and warm.

But tonight—last night, the night before, how many nights has it been?—I don't feel comforted by his presence. Instead, it makes me feel more alone. Asleep, he's a million miles away from me. Awake, he's even more distant. He lectures me, telling me what I should do, how I should feel. If he asks me how I am, he wants to hear that I'm fine. He doesn't want to hear anything else.

Sometimes at night I dream that I'm out in the middle of the prairie where I grew up. The sky and earth stretch on forever, making me smaller and smaller, a dot on the horizon. I'm standing there, waiting to disappear and escape from all of this. Waiting to be taken away.

Rory's sick the next day. Again. This is probably her fourteenth absence this semester. At the rate she's going, she's not going to graduate with the rest of us.

So I go ahead and have lunch with Beverly and Emma, even though it makes me uncomfortable. I don't know what I'm going to do when Rory comes back to school. Maybe I can change my lunch period so I can eat with some of my other friends. Lots of them have second-period lunch. It would be nice to see them. Maybe I wouldn't get indigestion around them, the way I have been with Beverly and Emma and Rory. Stress while you're eating is bad for you. I heard that on ABC News last week. It's better to have an empty stomach when something bad is happening.

"Where's your little friend, Liza?" Beverly asks when I walk up with my tray. "Is she pregnant again? Or is it some kind of venereal disease this time?"

Beverly's usually a lot more subtle than this. Her face is scrunched down, and she looks mean today. Her eyes are bloodshot, I notice, and she has red blotches on her cheeks. She looks like she stayed up all night crying. I guess I must be staring at her, because she drops her eyes to her plate and tries to hide her face.

"She has the flu, Beverly. Everybody's got it. Half the kids in my English class were gone today." Even though Beverly looks terrible, I know I sound sharper than I usually do.

Right now, I feel like I'm changing a lot. I never used to talk so sharply. That's not the kind of person I am. I used to be a nice, well-balanced, extremely confident person. I liked that.

Now I'm a sharp-tongued neurotic who jumps all over people who are her friends—except she's not even sure who her friends are, and almost faints when she sees her mother's surgery scars, and wants to kill her sister most of the time, and almost ran a stop light and got yelled at by a driver's ed maniac.

I always thought your personality was supposed to be formed by the time you were fifteen. What's happened to mine? It used to be great. Now, it's falling apart.

"You *hear* what happened in Saperstein's English class this morning?" Emma asks. "Jordan Everett got sent home for wearing a red shirt."

"What?" I ask. "Somebody thought Jordan Everett was in a gang? How dumb can they get?"

Jordan Everett's probably the most pious guy in our whole high school. He goes to the same church Beverly does, and his father's the minister. You know how preacher's kids are supposed to be wild and crazy? Well, somebody forgot to tell Jordan. He acts more like he's middle-aged than a teenager. He's already starting to bald just a lit-tle bit on the top of his head.

"Too bad," Emma says. She makes a loud slurping sound with her straw. "He should have remembered. Twelve kids got sent home yesterday for wearing red. Just because Jordan isn't the *gang* type doesn't mean the rules shouldn't apply to him."

Ever since Mrs. Thomas sent that memo out, it's become kind of famous. The local newspaper wrote about it, and the headline said, *Better Red Than Dead*. The reporter talked to two or three psycholo-gists about the negative effects on kids' self-esteem when they couldn't dress the way they wanted to. Then he talked to a lawyer about the students' Constitutional right to wear the color red. It was a pretty critical article.

Ariel loved it. She highlighted a lot of the nasty remarks people made about Mrs. Thomas and stuck it up on the bulletin board. Then she wrote, *Journalism Students of Houston High: Do We Really Want This Lunatic to Represent Us to the Rest of the World?*

Five minutes after she put it up, Mr. Sorensen pulled it down. That was after Ariel had left the room, and I don't think she's noticed it yet.

"You have to apply the same rules to everyone," Beverly's say-ing. "Rules are important. You can't make exceptions."

"I don't have that much red, anyway," Emma says. "My mother had me analyzed one time, and I'm a summer. You know—that means I'm not even supposed to wear red in the first place. It makes my skin look yellow." She tosses back her hair and grins at Beverly. "I think you're a summer, too, Beverly."

Beverly looks pleased, like Emma's given her a big compliment. She smiles back at Emma, and her face flushes. They look so satisfied with themselves—so smug and happy and superior and hateful that all of a sudden, something ugly rises up in me. It feels like vomit, only worse. I want to slap Beverly and Emma. Scream at them. Shake them till their fucking faces smash on the floor.

They think life is so simple, that's it. That's what I hate about both of them. Life is simple and easy and it makes sense. Even though Beverly's life is falling apart she still believes it. Follow the rules. Try hard. Do your best. Don't wear red. Don't dress like a slut, the way Rory does. Make the honor roll. Date a jock. Date another jock, if the first one dumps you. Don't ask too many questions. Don't look at life too carefully, or it'll scare the holy fucking bejeezus out of you.

Everything will be all right. Doesn't Beverly understand that might not be true? How can she be so goddamn dumb? Her life is a mess. Hasn't she noticed? What's wrong with her? And Emma's nuts, too. I'm pretty sure about that. Her whole family is crazy. Her mother got drunk last year and backed her new Volvo into a trash can at one o'clock in the morning.

I stare at my spaghetti and twirl it around on my fork. Then I take my knife and scrape it off the fork and cut it into little wormy pieces. I cut it so hard that I make jittery white marks on the plastic plate.

I can't do this any longer, I realize. I can't be around Beverly or Emma any better than Rory can. They're driving me crazy. They've got so many problems they can't even *see*, for God's sake. They're so stupid and blind and deluded that I almost feel sorry for them. It's pathetic, when you think about it. They're worse off than most of the people who write me for advice.

I scrape off the last bit of spaghetti and drag my knife across it. The plate looks battered, but I can see my reflection in between the scratches.

Self-absorption. That's what we talk about sometimes in our support group. We talk about how being sick can make you so minutely self-involved that nothing and no one else exists for you. All you care about is your own pain and disease.

Your world shrinks to the size of your body—which is being endlessly analyzed on scans, ultrasounds, blood measures, and tumor markers. The only thing that expands is your medical file. It looks like the Manhattan phone directory.

I try to pull myself away from all that—from my illness and fears— and go out into the world and look around. But it's so goddamn painful to see what's there. I want to go back and forget everything I've seen.

I'm causing them pain—Will and Liza and Jane. I've separated myself from them as much as they have from me. We're all trying to save ourselves—and each other—by the distance we're keeping. We don't want to hurt more than we're already hurting.

I watch Will at night. Lately, he's thrashing in his sleep. I see it in Jane's face. She looks as if she's bruised invisibly, trying to absorb what's happening to all of us.

I don't see it in Liza so much, and that worries me even more. She's holding on too tight, trying to hold on to something that's not there any longer.

She has to let go, somehow. I try to tell her that. But she doesn't hear me. She just goes on, moving forward, the way she always has.

Every day, I see Richard, and every night, he calls me and we talk. I've never spent so much time on the phone with a guy before.

Most of them speak in one-syllable words. You can tell they're dying to get off the phone the minute they get on so they can watch the World Series or something even more boring.

But Richard isn't like that. He loves to talk, speaking in that slow, husky voice. I could listen to it forever. Sometimes, I feel like I can almost see it, stretching out over me, like velvet that's unfolding. That sounds very exaggerated. But when I'm around Richard, I start exaggerating about everything. I can't help it.

Most nights, I lie on my bed and talk to him. He usually calls late, after I've finished my homework and taken a shower and I'm all wrapped up in my bathrobe. My whole room smells of shampoo and body lotion and warm skin. One night, I opened my curtains and shutters and let the moonlight come in while we talked. It made my bedspread and bathrobe look shiny and white and shimmery.

"You weren't asleep, were you?" Richard asks sometimes.

Of course not, I always tell him. The truth is, there's no way I could go to sleep while I'm waiting for him to call. But I don't tell him that.

He's very sensitive. That's what I really like about him. He can always tell what kind of mood I'm in by the way I talk. Nobody else does that. Nobody else even notices that I have moods these days.

Some nights, I feel like we're lying here, whispering secrets to each other, and we're the only two people on earth. We're in some kind of cocoon together, pulling closer and closer, wrapping our lives around each other and shutting out everything else. Nothing else matters. The rest of the world is crazy and loud and scary, but I don't care anymore. I can go to where it's dark and warm and safe. That's how I feel talking to Richard—safe. He'll take care of me. I know he will. I've never needed that before. But right now, I need it more than anything.

I can't even tell all the things we talk about, because we stay on the phone so long that I can't remember everything we say. He tells me about how his father's gone for several days in a row, because he's a pilot for one of the big airlines. While his dad's out of town, Richard stays by himself. "I don't like it," he says. "But after a while, I've gotten used to it."

His mother is still in Atlanta, and he misses her. "She's beautiful and smart," he says. "She started her own design company years ago—and she's a big success. Bigger than Dad is. I think that got to him."

"A lot of men in their generation are like that," I say. That's what Dad's always told me. Lots of men are threatened by a woman's success.

Richard's parents never told him why his father got custody of him and his mother didn't when they got divorced five years ago. He used to ask them, and they said it wasn't something they wanted to talk about. So he just stopped asking.

I think it must be terrible to have your parents divorce, but I don't say much about that. Lots of kids at school have parents who have split up, and I've always been glad that mine aren't. It must be awful to watch, kind of like seeing something you love torn up right in front of your eyes.

But I don't say that. I talk to Richard a lot, but there are plenty of things I don't tell him. Like how much I love his voice and how it seems to wrap itself around me and squeeze me all over till I feel like the whole world is warm and magical—the same way I felt when he kissed me. I don't want him to know that. But I think he knows it, anyway. Sometimes people know things, even though you haven't told them.

I even want to tell him about Mom being sick—but I can't. Not yet. Rory's still the only person I've told, and she hasn't told anybody. That's because people are so weird about cancer. All you have to do is say the word, and they go bananas. They treat you differently. They act like cancer's contagious or something, like you're carrying around a bunch of bad luck and they don't want to be around you. I'll tell Richard about it sometime, when everything's gotten a lot better. But right now, it's too soon. I'm going to wait.

It always takes me a long time to get to sleep after Richard and I hang up. Fortunately, I don't seem to need as much sleep as I used to, though. So I roll around on my bed and turn off the light, and it's dark and quiet and warm. I think about Richard. I try to think about lots of other important things—but I always end up thinking about him. At night. In my classes. At lunch. At dinner. It's all the same. I can't stop it.

Last fall, I answered a letter from a girl. She didn't sign her real name. She signed it "Madly in Love and Can't Help Myself"—like someone who was writing to Ann Landers or Dear Abby. *I've never been in love before. I want to be with him all the time. He's the only thing I think about. I can't control myself when I'm around him.* It went on and on like that, kind of like one of those bad teenage heartbreak songs.

The letter made me sad. It was clear to me that this girl was losing control and she might make some terrible mistake or get her heart broken and try to commit suicide. I mean, the letter was that passionate and crazy.

So I wrote her back and tried to remind her how young she was. She was only in high school, and you fall in love all the time when you're in high school. I said that—even though I'd never fallen in love. But I knew a lot of kids did. I told her she had to remember what was important—doing well in school, going on to college, preparing for the future. She had to take care of herself. She couldn't lose control the way she seemed to be doing.

Two or three weeks later, I got another note. I know it was from the same girl, even though she didn't sign it. It was written on the

135

same kind of notebook paper, and the handwriting was almost the same. But this time, it was bigger and looser, like she didn't care how it looked.

The note said, *I wish I hadn't written you. You don't understand at all.*

That's all there was. It made me feel terrible. It's the worst thing that's happened to me since I started writing the "Dear Deborah" advice column. I even thought about resigning after that. But Mr. Sorensen tried to talk me out of it. He said that something like that was inevitable. People wouldn't always like me or my advice, and I had to get used to that.

"It goes with the turf, Liza," he said. "You have to learn you can't do everything for everyone. It's impossible. You're human, you know." So I kept on writing the column, and, for a long time, I haven't gotten any awful letters like that one.

But ever since I've been around Richard, I've been thinking about that girl a lot. She was right. I didn't understand what she was telling me at all.

But now I do. When I listen to Richard, and my stomach gets tight and everything in me turns warm, I understand everything she was trying to tell me. And sometimes that scares me to death.

❧❧❧ ❧❧❧ ❧❧❧

Wednesday night, after I've talked to Richard, I can't go to sleep. I lie in my bed for a while, looking at the ceiling. It's one of those nights when the moon's really bright. It's almost like daylight in my room.

Dad told me once that milk has some kind of chemical that helps you get to sleep. So I go to the kitchen and heat up some milk on the stove. I'm about to carry it upstairs when I see Mom sitting in the living room in the dark.

"Are you okay?" I ask her. My eyes are finally accustomed to the shadows, and I can see her face. It looks soft and peaceful. Happy, almost. She's sitting on the leather couch with her feet under her hips. There's a glass of wine sitting on the coffee table in front of her.

"I'm all right, babe," she says. She reaches out her hand toward me. "Do you want to sit down and talk for a few minutes? We used to talk so much, Liza. I miss that."

I walk across the room and sit down beside Mom. I put my head on her shoulder. It feels thin. She must have lost even more weight after the surgery.

"I don't even know what's going on with you these days, Liza," Mom says. She smoothes my hair back and kisses me on the temple. "You're always so busy. But I miss talking to you. How are things going?"

How are things going? I don't know. The truth is, they're not going that well. Sometimes, I feel like my life's falling apart, and I don't know what to do about it. But I can't say that to Mom. She needs to be getting stronger right now. She needs every bit of strength she can gather for the stem-cell transplant, Dad says. She doesn't need to hear about my stupid problems. I should be able to take care of my own life.

So I tell Mom about how Mrs. Thomas banned the color red and how the food in the school cafeteria still sucks and what a bad teacher Ms. Reynolds is. I tell her all the things in my life that are funny and aren't important. I try to make her laugh. I want to see her laugh, since it's been a long time. Laughter is supposed to be really good for you when you're sick. I've read studies about that.

But Mom doesn't seem very amused by my stories. She listens very quietly, and sometimes she strokes my hair and pats me on the shoulder. But she doesn't say much. I don't know why. After I've finished telling the stories and laughing at them myself, it's quiet in the room.

Finally, Mom starts to talk. She tells me how much she hates being sick again and how much she hates the thought of getting more treatment and feeling helpless.

It's one of those times when Mom's talking faster and faster, like she's afraid she won't get to tell me everything she needs to say. She talks about how having cancer has made her want to live differently—more fully—because she's not sure how long she has to live.

"It's funny—but everything seems simpler after you've been diagnosed with cancer," she says. "It's scary—but there aren't that many other things I'm afraid of. Sometimes, I want to talk to you about that so you'll understand. I want you to understand this, babe. It's not all bad.

"Sometimes, it feels like I've gone into a great dark place. You know what that's like. It takes a while for your eyes to adjust. But after they do, you see things . . . you see things you've never seen before."

The more she talks, the more I can feel some kind of panic rising in me, like a siren that's going off. I can't let Mom talk like this. I've got to stop her. She's letting herself get scared and depressed. This is terrible. There's no way she's going to get well if she's acting like this. She's thinking about all the bad things that can happen. She's not thinking about anything that's good.

"It's going to be all right, Mom," I say. I try to make my voice as calm as possible. I have to get some kind of control over this before everything gets worse. Before you know it, Mom's going to be talking about how cancer can kill you. She doesn't need to be thinking like that, and she sure as hell doesn't need to be talking like it. It's too negative. It's dangerous. "I know it. I know it's going to be all right."

Mom pulls back and stares at me. She touches my hair again and kisses me on the cheek. "You've got to go to bed, babe. You need your sleep." She kisses me again and draws back. Something in her face has changed. It's tight and sad, all of a sudden, like a mask. She's gone away and left me again, and I don't know why.

Even in the dark, her eyes are beautiful and blue and far away from me. What happened? Where's she going? Why can't she stay here?

Tonight, I wanted so much to take Liza's face in my hands and scream at her, whisper to her, make her listen to every word so she'll understand me, know what I know. I want us to talk deeply, continually, directly from our hearts. I don't want us to say anything that isn't important and real.

We don't have time to waste. We have to love each other as much as we can, say everything that needs to be said. Can't she or Jane understand that? Can't Will? Why am I the only one?

They look at me, so often, with pity or alarm. How can they pity me, goddamnit? Can't they see how much I've changed—how different I am?

The week goes on. It's getting closer and closer to Christmas, but something's wrong. I can feel it every time I come in the front door. Something's wrong. Mom and Dad are acting strange around each other.

Like I said, they've always gotten along great. They hardly ever have arguments. But now everything's different.

When they're in the same room, they don't talk as much as they used to. Sometimes, they don't even look at each other. Mostly, it's Dad looking at Mom and talking to her and trying to help her. But Mom doesn't act the way she used to. She seems angry at Dad sometimes. That's crazy, but it's the way she's acting. Some days, Dad will say things to her, and she won't even answer for a long, long time. It's awful when that happens, like all that silence is a knife that's ripping us apart. I want to jump in and start talking about something—anything—so there won't be that long, horrible silence.

Jane notices it, too. I can tell. Even though she's extremely self-involved and immature, she looks worried when she's around Mom and Dad. She pulls on her hair a lot. She always does that when she's nervous. Sometimes, she tries to talk about things at school, like her Davy Crockett project. But it isn't like she enjoys talking about it. She acts as nervous as I am. She just starts babbling so there will be sounds somewhere and we won't have to listen to the silence.

"Do you know Hispanics have a very different view of the Alamo than Anglos do?" That's what Jane is saying at dinner tonight. She acts like it was a big historical discovery that she'd just made.

"Really?" I'm trying to act like I'm very interested, and this is some kind of breaking news story. Jane's face gets happier when I say that, and she starts talking about how the Texas Revolution is being looked at by all kinds of people. Views are changing and people are taking a multicultural approach.

"It's not like it was when you were growing up, Mom and Dad," Jane says.

Mom's sitting at the dinner table, but she isn't eating. She's just staring out the window, even though it's dark outside. Dad's not eating that much, either. He's watching Mom and he looks worried. Neither of them says anything to answer Jane.

So she turns to Granddad and says in an even louder voice, "A lot of things about history are changing, Granddad."

Granddad is the only one at the table who's eating. When he finally notices Jane's talking to him, he frowns while he drags his bread around the plate to pick up anything that's left. He lived through the Depression, Mom and Dad say, which is why he never leaves anything on his plate. "How can history change, hon? It's already over with."

"It's hard to explain, Granddad," Jane says.

I've been angry with Jane for the past few days, but tonight, I feel sorry for her. She's trying so hard to talk and act like things are normal. So she goes on talking, telling Granddad about how all the different ethnic groups have a different point of view, and we should respect all of them. I don't think Granddad even hears much of what she's saying, fortunately. He's one of those unicultural people.

I know I should be talking, too, and trying to make things better. But I just feel sick to my stomach. The more I look at the food on my plate, the worse I feel. But it's better than watching Dad and Mom and trying to understand what's going on with them. What's wrong with them, anyway? I've never seen them act like this before. They've always been so crazy about each other. When did this start? What's wrong?

It's all so bad that Jane and I actually offer to do the dishes after dinner. She rinses the plates and I put them in the dishwasher. We make so much noise with the water and banging plates around that we can't hear anything else, and we don't have to talk. It takes us about fifteen minutes, since we're not really that great about cleaning up the kitchen. But finally, everything looks pretty good, so we

141

turn off the water and start the dishwasher. It's one of those new, quieter dishwashers. After we turn it on, we can hear a lot better.

Dad and Mom are yelling at each other upstairs. That's something I've never heard before in my life. I listen, even though I don't want to. I can't stop myself.

"You've changed." That's Dad talking. "You've changed so much, Rebecca—I don't even recognize you some days."

"I *wanted* to change. I'm glad I've changed."

For a few minutes, I can't hear what they're saying. Then they start talking louder again. They're yelling at each other about hope. *Hope?* How can that be? You can't argue about hope, can you? How can you? There's nothing to argue about. You should always have hope. Everybody knows that.

"You can't give up hope, Rebecca," Dad is saying. His voice sounds terrible, like he's about to cry. But that's crazy. He never cries.

"I haven't given up hope, Will," Mom says. Her voice is louder than it's been in years. It's even louder than Dad's. We can hear every word she's saying, like she's slapping Dad and Jane and me across our faces, as hard as she can. But *why?* Why's she doing this to us? Doesn't she know we love her? "Goddamnit—don't tell me I've given up hope. But I'm not hoping for the same thing you are. I'm hoping for something else. Can't you understand that? Why can't you listen to me?"

I stand there, wiping my hands on the dish towel. Jane and I are standing there, like we're frozen. But we don't look at each other, and we don't say anything. When I finally glance at her, she has her eyes shut.

❦ ❦ ❦

The next morning, the weather's finally gotten cold. The sky is gray and heavy, and there's a thin, sharp wind that touches every

142

part of your body and makes you shiver. It doesn't usually get this cold in Austin, believe me.

When I get to my locker, everyone's standing around reading the school newspaper. That's great. I've never seen so many people reading the newspaper before. In fact, it's kind of weird.

I see a few groups that are reading something out loud and then they're laughing at it. Uh-oh. That's not a good sign. I guess we must have made some kind of big, dumb mistake. Some of the other kids just love it when we make big mistakes. It's a very destructive attitude. They should try working on a newspaper themselves, instead of standing around, criticizing it. It's hard to put out a newspaper, but I don't think anybody knows that.

I grab a paper and head up the stairs to Richard's locker. He's standing in front of it, rubbing the back of his neck. He has fine, soft hair on the back of his neck that makes him look innocent, like he's just a kid. But he's taller than I am, and his muscles look strong and hard.

"Are you ogling me, Liza?" he asks. "I think you were."

I know I'm turning red, because my face feels hot. I hate to blush. It makes me feel like a lovesick idiot. I let my hair fall in my face so it won't be so noticeable. Then I scoop it back over my shoulders. I've been trying not to play with my hair so much or toss it around when I'm with Richard. But it's better than just standing there with a face as red as a stop sign.

"What an ego," I say. "I could have been looking at somebody else. Why d'you think it's you?"

He grins and clutches my arm while we walk down the hall. "I didn't realize how dangerously you journalists like to live. I can't believe you actually printed that column Ariel Lowenthal wrote." He whistles. "There's gonna be H-E-double-L to pay."

"What are you talking about?"

I feel like I'm in an elevator that's out of control. I'm at the top of some building and we're going down fast. I feel sick. *Ariel's column.* It was about Mrs. Thomas's outlawing red. I was supposed to read it that afternoon, before it went to the printer. I told Mr. Sorensen I would. But I didn't. I forgot all about it. I never even saw it.

My God. What's in it? Is it too late to take the newspapers back?

"Shit, shit, shit," I say. "Fuck. Goddamnit. Let me see what it says."

"Such foul language from such a wholesome girl," Richard says.

I rip the paper open and stand there in the hall while I read it. People are pouring around me, laughing and talking, and a few of them bump into me. When I finally get to the page I want, I walk along slowly.

There's Ariel's picture. Other people look embarrassed when they get their picture taken. But not Ariel. She loves it when the whole world's focused on her. She's staring right at the camera, grinning up through her glasses. They have rhinestones in them, and they sparkle, even in the picture.

"Liza! Get a move on. The bell's ringing." Richard guides me through the halls, and I stuff the paper under my arm till we get to French. When we get there, I don't look at Rory or anyone else. I just sink into my seat and hunch over so Ms. Reynolds won't see me. I fold the paper so it's really small and I can read Ariel's column.

I try to take long, slow breaths and calm down. Maybe it's not as bad as I think it is. Maybe. But I know that's crazy. Of course it is. Ariel would never pass up a chance like this.

A Student's View: Stop the Insanity!

I can remember when I was in middle school. I could hardly wait till I got to high school with the big kids, so I could have more freedom and express myself.

Now, when I think back to that time, I laugh. I was such an idiot! The truth is, at Sam Houston High School, students have a lot less freedom than kids at the worst middle school in the city. Maybe in the world.

In her latest emotional tantrum, our esteemed principal has decreed that students at our high school can't wear the color red. Mrs. Ann Thomas, who is known to most students by the nickname "The Menopause Queen," has now officially gone nuts. If students don't wear red, her "logic" appears to be, they will not join gangs. What could be more simple? What could be dumber? This is the desperate act of someone who is rapidly losing her grip on reality.

I can hardly wait till Mrs. Thomas's next brainstorm. Maybe she'll decide that if people don't wear blue, they won't get cancer. Or if we don't wear plaid, there won't be any more wars and the hole in the ozone layer will disappear. The list could go on and on—but frankly, I hate to give her more ideas.

In the meantime, SHHS students are left with lots of perplexing questions. When is a color really red—and when is it hot pink or orange or mauve? Can you wear red fingernail polish or lipstick? (If you're a girl, of course. Our high school is also big-time homophobic, but that's another problem we should deal with later.) What if you have red hair? What if you start bleeding? What if you get a really bad sunburn or your eyes are bloodshot?

In Mrs. Thomas's tiny little world, our national flag would be blue and white, and so would our state flag. Santa Claus would wear green. What's next?

I urge all students to join me in boycotting this ridiculous policy of a madwoman. On Friday, let's all pull together—and wear everything that's red in our closets. Power to the students! Stop the insanity!

That's it. Oh, my God. I feel dizzy. I'm close to falling on the floor and staying there. Except I might have to vomit first. *Madwoman? The Menopause Queen? Losing her grip on reality?* Mrs. Thomas doesn't like the slightest bit of criticism. What's she going to do when she sees this? I don't want to know. I get even sicker to my stomach just thinking about it.

For the rest of the class, I slump in my seat and hope Ms. Reynolds doesn't notice. I don't think she does. She's too busy trying to learn a few French words so she can teach them to us.

I look back down at the column, and I feel sick again. All I can think about is Mr. Sorensen. This is all my fault. Every bit of it. Ariel always needs someone around to control her. I know that just as well as Mr. Sorensen does. And I was the person he trusted to make sure something like this wouldn't happen. I let everybody down—especially him.

I don't want to go near the journalism office. I'm sure I'll find his body there or something. If there's a knife in it, it should probably have my name on it.

❧ ❧ ❧

The rest of the day, it's like waiting for a tornado to hit. It's like it is when the skies are black and green and the air's still and the sirens are wailing and you know something terrible's about to happen. So you go in a closet and pull a pillow over your head and wait.

That's what it's like at school today. Everyone's waiting for Mrs. Thomas to do something. To seize all the newspapers and get on the intercom and shut down the school. Or something worse. But so far, she hasn't done anything. Nobody's even seen her.

It's like waiting for a tornado to hit, except it isn't nearly that quiet. People are still standing around, pointing and laughing at

146

the newspaper. They're even treating Ariel like some kind of celebrity. That's weird. Hardly anyone has ever paid attention to Ariel, except for people on the newspaper. Now she seems to have a spotlight on her. She looks happier than I've ever seen her. She's also avoiding me. She knows she should have reminded me to look at her column, and she didn't. She didn't want to. She knew I would have tried to stop her.

Ariel and I don't see each other the whole day, till classes are over. That's when we run into each other in front of the journalism room.

"I guess you're mad at me, Liza," Ariel says. "I guess I owe you an apology." She doesn't look sorry, though. Her eyes are bright, like she has some kind of fever, and she keeps grinning even when nothing's going on.

I don't like apologies. I hate to make them and I hate to get them. They're embarrassing. I wish we'd all just act right in the first place so we wouldn't have to apologize for anything.

"It's not me I'm worried about," I say. "It's Mr. Sorensen. He could lose his job over this, Ariel. Don't you ever think about anybody but yourself?"

Ariel pulls back a little and glares at me. "I wasn't thinking about myself. I was thinking about the whole school. Sometimes you have to stand up to authority."

Oh, please. Ariel's not a bad person—not really. At least I don't think she is. But she doesn't care about principles, either. She just wants everyone to pay attention to her. She'll do anything to get that. I know she didn't mean to hurt Mr. Sorensen or me. But she also didn't want to think about us when she had a chance to do something important. It would never have occurred to her that not hurting someone else was more important than something she wanted to do.

147

We walk in the room, and Mr. Sorensen's sitting there at his desk. He's got his head bent down and he's reading something. He's beginning to go bald on top of his head, in a little circle that's sunburned. I've never noticed that before. His shoulders are slumped. He doesn't look jaunty, the way he used to. He looks worn out.

Mr. Sorensen looks up and sees Ariel and me. Then he sighs.

Ariel steps up right in front of his desk. She's arching her body like she's a big rubber band, and she has her hand by her eyes, like she's about to wipe away a bunch of tears. "Mr. Sorensen, I feel terrible about this whole mess," she says. She acts like she's been in agony the whole day, instead of floating around in the middle of a bunch of crowds, gloating and laughing. "I don't know what got into me." She sniffs very loudly. It's not very convincing. It's pathetic, as a matter of fact.

Mr. Sorensen purses his lips. He doesn't seem upset or depressed, the way I thought he'd be. He looks calm. Not jaunty, not happy—but calm. I don't know why. Maybe he's on some kind of medication or something. Maybe he's just taken a big overdose and he's going to fall over on the floor and we'll have to call 911. I know a little CPR, but I've never had to use it. If he dies, it will be my fault. Mine and Ariel's. But I'm the only one who'll feel guilty about it.

"You don't need to go into all of that with me, Ariel," he says. "Save all your theatrics for Mrs. Thomas. She'd like to see you right now."

Ariel almost grins when she hears that. I'm sure she's been waiting to get hauled into the principal's office the whole day. She'd love to get kicked out of school and go to court. She told me once that was kind of her high-school goal. If she gets expelled from school on a First Amendment issue, that's what she can write about on her college essay.

"Is this serious?" she asks.

Mr. Sorensen is staring down at his book again. He shrugs. "It depends on what you consider serious, Ariel." That's not the kind of thing teachers are supposed to say to students. Mr. Sorensen is acting very strange today.

"Do you want to go with me, Mr. Sorensen?" Ariel asks.

"That won't be necessary, Ariel. I've already had a nice, long talk with Mrs. Thomas."

Ariel leaves, and Mr. Sorensen and I are the only two people left in the room. It's so quiet in here. I wish he would say something, instead of staring at his book. Can he really be reading with all of this going on? Has he forgotten I'm in the room, too? No, of course not. What am I thinking of? How could he forget?

I take off my backpack and sit down at the desk in front of his. I'm making a lot of noise, but he doesn't look up. So I clear my throat. I feel like somebody's got his hand around my neck. It's hard to breathe or talk.

"Mr. Sorensen, I—"

He looks up at me and I stop. His eyes are light brown. They're gentle and kind, like the rest of him. I've never noticed. I guess I've never looked him in the eyes before. I wonder what I've been looking at, instead. I thought I was good at looking people in the face when I talked to them. But maybe I'm not. I thought I saw things clearly. But maybe I don't. Maybe I don't see anything at all that's important.

Mr. Sorensen closes his book and puts his hands on top of it. His face is sad, but he doesn't seem angry. I wish he was. I wish he'd throw his book at the wall or scream or walk out of the room. Anything would be better than having him look at me like this.

"Mr. Sorensen, I—I don't know what to say. I forgot to read Ariel's column. I don't have any excuse. I just forgot."

I shut my eyes. I can't even look at him while I talk. Besides, I

149

know why I forgot. I saw Richard that afternoon, and I couldn't think of anything else. If I'd been doing anything important—like being a lifeguard or a baby-sitter or a doctor in surgery—I would have done the same thing. I'm not the kind of person everybody can depend on. That was just something I liked to believe about myself. But I was wrong. The truth is, I'm not even a better person than Ariel. At least she had some kind of reason for doing what she did. I didn't have any kind of reason at all. I was just out of control, crazy, in love, or whatever you call it. I'd been everything I'd always tried not to be. Irresponsible. Immature. Destructive. If I acted like that, I'm not sure who I am anymore.

"I feel awful about this, Mr. Sorensen. You trusted me and I let you down. . . ." I want to say more, but it takes me ages to even speak. My mouth's not working the way it should. Neither is my brain. "I can't tell you how sorry I am."

It's quiet in the room again. Finally, Mr. Sorensen draws a big breath and lets it out. Actually, it's more like a wheeze.

"I know you didn't mean to hurt me, Liza. You're not that kind of person. I know that." He tries to smile at me, but he doesn't quite make it. But his eyes are still the same. Kind and gentle. "I also know that I gave you too much responsibility that day. That was my fault. You're only a high-school student—and I knew how much strain you had at home, with your mother being sick again."

Something grips my stomach, and I look at the floor. So Mr. Sorensen knows. He knows Mom's sick again.

He's right about that. But he's wrong to say it isn't my fault. Because it is. It's all my fault. I don't have any real excuses. Things at home aren't as bad as he's trying to make them sound. He's just exaggerating to try to make me feel better.

"But that doesn't make any difference, Mr. Sorensen. I'm not under that much strain—and I should never have—"

Mr. Sorensen puts up his hand and gestures for me to stop talking. "Liza, please. Can't we talk? I know how sick your mother is. And I know how much you're going to be going through with the stem-cell transplant. I know what that's like. I know how bad the odds are. I just wish you could have told me about it. I wish you'd let me be your friend. Why do you have to act so strong all the time? Don't you know how hard that is on you?"

Bad odds? Act so strong? What's he talking about?

"It's not that bad, Mr. Sorensen. You make it sound like it's hopeless—but it's not. It's a hard time, right now. But Mom's going to be fine. We're all going to be fine. Sure, it's hard—but it's no excuse for what I did."

For a few long seconds, Mr. Sorensen doesn't say anything. He has a pencil in his hands, and he watches while he rolls it around. His hands are thinner than the rest of him. They look like a pianist's hands, long and thin and graceful.

When he looks up again, there's something even sadder about him. What happened? What's wrong with him? He looks worse than he did before we started to talk today.

"Liza," he says. "Don't do this to yourself. Please. Don't."

I can understand the look on his face. Finally. Now I see it. I came in here to apologize. But he's the one who feels sorry for me. How did that happen? How on earth did that happen? What in the hell does he mean by it?

I gather up my backpack and run out of the room.

❄❄❄ ❄❄❄ ❄❄❄

"You're late, Liza. As usual."

Mr. Bridges doesn't even say hello anymore. Today, he looks even more irritated at me than usual. He holds up his stopwatch and lets it dangle in the air. "You are exactly four minutes and fifty-three seconds late. Frank and I thought you weren't going to show up."

"I'm sorry." I left the house early enough, but Granddad wanted to drive me here. That took forever. That's why I'm late. I'm almost never late to anything. But I never get to driver's ed on time, for some reason.

"You first, Liza," Mr. Bridges says when we get to the car. He opens the driver's door for me. "We'll get the worst part over with," he says in a lower voice to Frank. Frank laughs. I guess they don't think I can hear them. Or maybe they want me to hear them, so I'll feel bad. But I don't know how I could feel much worse than I do now.

I sit up straight and pretend like I know what I'm doing. When I change lanes, I signal. I'm going exactly one mile under the speed limit, which is what you're supposed to do, in case your speedometer's wrong. I try to brake very smoothly, so you can't even feel it in the car.

In fact, I think I'm doing pretty well. But Mr. Bridges doesn't seem to notice. He's turning around, talking to Frank most of the time. They're talking about basketball or something, and every time one of them says something, they both laugh. I don't know why. I never hear them say anything funny.

"Turn left, Liza." Mr. Bridges finally turns around to me and points. I wish he'd keep on talking to Frank. When he watches me, he always finds something wrong. I wouldn't mind that if he said anything nicely. But he doesn't. He just starts to pick on me for little things, and then he ends up yelling. It's terrible when that starts to happen. But I can't do anything to stop it. "We're going to practice some freeway driving today."

"She's getting nervous," Frank says from the backseat. "Look at her shoulders."

152

I've always hated it when he talked *to* me. But I hate it even worse when he talks *about* me—like I'm not even here.

I drive up a hill, past a lot of trees and big houses. Then I pull onto the entrance ramp. It's a fairly new freeway, and the ramp is long and gradual. Right now, it's crowded on the road. All I can see are red taillights moving along smoothly.

"God, this traffic's gotten worse since them damned Californians moved here," Mr. Bridges says. He rolls down the window and spits. I don't think a driver's ed teacher should do that. It's not polite at all. Also, his grammar stinks. "Guess that don't bother you, though, Liza. Since you're a doctor's daughter and you live in the ritzy part of the city and all that. Don't have to fight the traffic getting into town. Not like the rest of us rednecks."

How does he know where I live? What does he know about me? How does he know what Dad does, anyway? Is that why he hates me so much—because he thinks I'm rich? Maybe that's it. He hates everything about me. Everything.

"Get outta this righthand lane fast," Mr. Bridges says. He shifts in the seat and moves his coffee to his other hand. "You're not supposed to stay here."

I signal, but the lane next to me is full. So I slow down a little and keep my turn-signal indicator on. That's what you're supposed to do, I think. I keep peering into the rearview mirror, trying to find an opening.

"Speed up, Liza. This is a freeway, for God's sake. You're going too slow. You're never gonna get over if you're going this slow."

I press on the accelerator. Then I notice an opening in the traffic in the left lane. I yank the steering wheel and we lurch into the next lane. Mr. Bridges spills coffee all over his blue jeans.

"Goddamnit to hell, Liza! Didn't I tell you a driver should always move smoothly?"

153

I glance at his lap. His blue jeans are darker where the coffee's spilled, and he's mopping it up with a napkin. It must be hot, because he's swearing up a storm, and his face is bright red. It's awful.

I can't do anything right these days. Not when I'm around anybody. It's not just Mr. Bridges. It's the whole world. I'm messing up everywhere. It doesn't matter how hard I try.

I look back at the road, just in time to see the traffic's not moving any longer. I've always heard that time expands when something terrible happens. It must be true, since it seems to take us forever to hit the car in front of us.

❧ ❧ ❧

I flunked driver's ed. That's what Mr. Bridges tells me when we finally get back to the driving school. He thinks I'm the only student in the history of the Driving Safe-T school who's ever totaled a car while she's under instruction.

"I'll be checking the records to make sure," he says. "We like to know when our students do something that's never been done before."

Mr. Bridges grins at me. It's not a friendly grin, either. I don't know what a friendly grin would look like on his face.

He's not hurt—and neither was Frank or I or anybody else. It was just that the car kind of got smashed up.

We ran into a red pickup truck. After we stopped, we all looked at the back of the truck, but we couldn't even find a scratch on it.

"Course not," the guy who owned the pickup truck said. "Why d'ya think people drive pickup trucks, anyway? 'Cause they want to haul bales of hay?" He even patted me on the shoulder. "Don't worry about it, hon. No harm done. Ever'body gets into wrecks sometimes."

I wish I'd had him for a driving instructor. He was so nice, he even dropped us off at the driving school after our car had been towed.

"You know how this school works, Liza," Mr. Bridges is saying. "You can take this course as many times as you need to. But why don't you try another driving instructor the next time?"

He grins at me, like he can hardly wait for me to leave so he can burst out laughing. It's weird what happens then. All of a sudden, I'm not scared of him any longer. I don't have that sick feeling in my stomach, just being around him. I feel so angry I want to kill him.

Why has Mr. Bridges treated me so badly? I've wondered that for a long time. But now, I'm wondering something else. Why had I *let* him treat me so badly? I'm not like this. I can take up for myself. I know what I would have said to any girl who'd written a letter to "Dear Deborah" about a driving instructor—or anyone else—who treated her like this. I would have told her to report him to somebody. Or tell her parents. Or sue for sexual discrimination. There are lots of lawyers around. That's what I would have told anybody. So why couldn't I see that in my own life? Why couldn't I do something that was so simple and obvious?

I'm so angry I can't talk. Maybe that's better. I shouldn't say anything. Mr. Bridges hands me some kind of paper and I snatch it away from him without saying anything. It practically whistles, going through the air.

"Be seeing you, Liza," he says.

But I don't answer. Mr. Bridges is only the second person I've ever hated in my life—after that Renee creature.

I walk out without saying anything and let the door slam. That's very dramatic for me.

"Ready, hon?" Granddad says. He didn't notice that we came

155

back in a different car. He switches the ignition on and his car starts to cough. The second time, it catches. Thank God. I would rather die than walk back into the driver's ed school and ask Mr. Bridges for a ride.

"I'm not going back there, Granddad. I just flunked driver's ed."

The minute I say that, I feel worse. All my anger leaves me, and I want to cry.

I've never flunked anything in my life. Not even a test. So this is what it feels like. It feels terrible. I feel like the biggest failure in the world. Nobody flunks driver's ed—except for me. I wonder if people at school will hear about it. Maybe I should resign from my column right now. Nobody wants to get advice from somebody who forgets to edit Ariel Lowenthal and gets her favorite teacher in trouble and flunks driver's ed. Why would they? Anybody's smarter than that. Anybody.

"It's okay, hon," Granddad says. He reaches over and pats me on the hand and the car almost hits a curb. "Most women can't drive worth beans, anyway. Even your grandma was a pretty bad driver. She ran into a cow one time. I ever tell you about that?"

Granddad keeps talking, and naturally, that slows down his driving even more. But at least he doesn't stop to listen to the radio. When we get to our house, he pulls in next to the curb and stops the car.

"Granddad—please don't tell anybody what I told you." I need time to think. Dad's going to be pretty upset about this. He doesn't need something else to worry about, with Mom going into the hospital next week.

Maybe I can just forget to tell Dad, till things get better. I'll look through the mail and intercept anything from the driving school. That way, maybe no one will even know I flunked driver's ed. I can just drive around without a license. That's what I'll do. As long as I don't get stopped by the police, I'll be fine.

Granddad turns to look at me. "What're you talking about, hon? What'd you tell me?"

❧❧❧ ❧❧❧ ❧❧❧

For the first time in three days, we actually sit down for a meal together. One of Mom's friends from her support group brings us barbecued chicken and potato salad. It's Barbara. I'm glad it's her. I like her more than anyone else in that group. As usual, she's smiling and she has lipstick on her teeth and she smells like fresh air. It always cheers me up to be around Barbara. I hope it cheers up Mom, too. Right now, she needs that.

I rinse off the plates Barbara brought the meal on and dry them off. It's always a lot better to do that immediately. Otherwise, you end up with a lot of plates and you don't know who they belong to and it's a big pain to take them back.

"Enjoy it!" Barbara says and waves.

I follow her to her car, carrying the plates. "Anywhere's fine," she says, pointing to her backseat. It's very messy, with lots of old newspapers and books piled up. "That plate's already pretty beaten-up. I always use it for meals for sick friends." Her voice dwindles off so it's quieter. "I've had lots of sick friends."

Barbara gets in the driver's seat and rolls down her window. For once, she's not smiling. "Liza, honey, I need to ask you something." She looks me straight in the eyes. "How are you—really? And how are Jane and your dad?"

"We're fine." I wish people would stop asking questions like that when they come to see us. They always ask the same thing, and

157

I always say the same thing. Why can't we all stop? "We know we have a few tough weeks coming up—with Mom's stem-cell transplant. But we're ready for it."

I try to make my voice sound stronger, like I'm making a speech. I don't want Barbara to think we're in denial. Sometimes people get that way, Dad says. They act like someone isn't even sick, and that's extremely dangerous behavior that worries doctors. That's not how my family is at all, and I want to make sure Barbara knows that. I don't want her to worry about us.

Barbara's still staring at me. I wish she wouldn't do that. It makes me feel like a little kid who's been caught doing something wrong. Why doesn't she stop acting like that? It's not like she's my mother or anything.

"Do you know what you're talking about, Liza? Do you really know?" She sighs and runs a finger along the top of her window glass, back and forth, like she's very nervous. "I know it isn't my place to talk about this—but it worries your mother. Do you know how serious a stem-cell transplant is? Do you . . . do you know how sick your mother really is?"

Why does she keep talking like this? Does she think I'm a five-year-old? "Of course I know. That's why she's doing the stem-cell. So she can get better." I try not to sound impatient. But Barbara's beginning to get on my nerves.

"But . . . but, Liza—it's not that simple. It doesn't always work. And it's a terrible thing to have to go through, and your mother is thinking—"

What's wrong with Barbara? She should be trying to make me feel better. But she's not. She's making me feel worse. I don't want to be around her. I was wrong about her. She's not a good person or a friend. She's one of those people who tries to make a tragedy out of everything. Someone who looks on the dark side of life. I wish she'd leave right now. I don't like her.

"You know, you can be too optimistic about things," Barbara's saying. "You can do that—but you're missing so much. . . . You're paying a bigger price than you know. You can't control everything. You can't—"

"It was so nice of you to bring dinner, Mrs. Watkins," I interrupt. Kids aren't supposed to interrupt adults, but I think I need to right now. "We all love barbecued chicken. Thank you so much."

I smile, but Barbara doesn't smile back. She just stares at me again for a few seconds, like she's trying to read something that's written on my face. It's a very odd thing to do. She opens her mouth to say something else, but then she closes it. She rolls up her window and starts her car and drives away. I feel better the minute her car turns the corner and I can't see it any longer.

I walk up the stone path to our front door and kick a few pebbles. The grass has turned brown, and I haven't even noticed it. I haven't been outside jogging that much lately.

Inside, Jane's already set the table without complaining. She even put out drinks for everybody. Ever since that night she and I heard Mom and Dad yelling at each other, she's been a lot better. She's been doing a lot of things around the house, even when Dad doesn't ask her to do them. Maybe she's finally growing up. I hope so.

The five of us sit down. Jane lights candles, as usual, and dims the lights. We smile at each other, but nobody says much.

Dad makes a big deal about passing the chicken around and saying how good it looks. I say that barbecued chicken is my favorite dish. I notice I'm speaking louder than I usually do, the same way Jane's been. I think I know why. I don't want Dad to start asking me

159

about driver's ed or about the school newspaper or Mr. Sorensen. If I keep talking about the meal, then he won't right now. I can wait to tell him when it's a better time.

"You cook this, Rebecca?" Granddad asks. He's picked up a piece of chicken, and the sauce is all over his face.

"A friend of Mom's brought it," Jane says. "You know—that woman who was just here. Barbara Watkins. Don't you remember, Granddad?"

"What friend?" Granddad says, frowning.

This could go on forever. Once Granddad starts asking questions, he'll go on till midnight. Tonight, I just don't feel like it.

So I start talking. I talk about Mr. Moffitt. It's a nice long story, which is good. I talk about how much everybody in our class last year loved him, and what Mr. Moffitt had taught us about the American Indians. I tell about Ray's report and how Mr. Moffitt acted, and how he didn't come back after Christmas break. Then I tell them what Ray learned about Mr. Moffitt—how he really wasn't an American Indian at all. He'd just pretended to be.

I go on and on. It takes me ages to finish the story. After it's over, Mom and Dad and Jane are all staring at me. Even Granddad looks kind of interested. It's the first thing all of us have done together in weeks, I realize. It feels like something exploded and sent us all into different directions. Even though we live together and eat together and ride in the car together, it doesn't feel like we're a family any longer. But now, for a few minutes we are. We're doing something together, in the same place, at the same time.

I wish I had other stories I could tell. I wish I could talk and talk and talk forever—and keep us all together, the way we are right now. I want to hold us so tight that we can't move.

But I can't think of any other stories. I've told the only one I know—talking on and on. And now I'm exhausted. I can't say anything more.

"So—your teacher lied?" Jane asks. "He wasn't really an Indian? Why did he do that?"

Mom cocks her head to one side. Then she shakes it slowly. She looks different tonight. She looks better than she has in ages—prettier and stronger and more alive. She must be getting better. That's it. She's getting ready to fight this thing, the way we all hoped she would. She seems more positive than I've seen her in a long time.

"You never know why people do the things they do," she says. "All we can ever do is guess. Maybe it made him feel like he was a part of something. Sometimes, you want other people to care about you so badly that you'll do anything. You'll be anything they want you to be."

Her words linger around us, like soft, warm air that touches you, even though you can't see it. For a few seconds, no one else speaks.

That's the way Mom is. I'd almost forgotten. She's quiet for a long time, and then she says something like that. It makes me think of what Dad said about her once. "Your mother understands things I can't even see. She always has." I remember how his face looked when he said that. I felt like I could look in his face and see all the love he had for Mom, the way he'd always felt about her. That made me feel strange and kind of embarrassed, the way I always am when I see how my parents feel about each other. After they've been yelling at each other so much, I wonder if they still feel that way. I don't know. I can't tell.

"Did the Indians really have slaves?" Jane asks.

I shrug. "That's what Ray says. He brought a bunch of books to show us after Mr. Moffitt left."

It makes me feel uncomfortable, just thinking about looking at those books. Even though I like Ray a lot, I wanted to see what Mr. Moffitt had told us—about all the beauty and tragedy of the Chickasaws, how he made us feel they were better than we were, stronger and more noble. It was nice to have something like that to believe in. It was nice to have someone like Mr. Moffitt to believe in, too, and to make us excited about school and what was wrong with the world. After it was gone, I missed it. Even if it was all a great, big lie, I still missed it.

Dad doesn't say anything. Not a word. Through the whole meal, he kept looking at Mom, glancing at her all the time. He seems jumpy, which is very odd. Dad's got a lot of energy, but he's never jumpy about anything. Granddad's not saying anything, either. He's too busy eating his chicken. All that's left on his plate is a bunch of tiny bones. It looks like he cleaned them off with a knife or something.

"What an unbelievable story, Liza—all of it." Mom's still shaking her head slowly. "I think it's one of the saddest things I've ever heard in my life. Someone should write a book about it."

A few years ago, one of us would have said Mom's the one who should write that book. But that was a long time ago. We don't say that anymore.

"What makes people lie like that?" Jane asks. She's not even interested in hearing more about the Indians. She keeps asking the same question over and over, like Mom hasn't already answered it.

Besides, she's missing the point. As usual. Mr. Moffitt hadn't lied—not really. He wasn't lying or "spinning" like all those political creeps in Washington my American history teacher is always talking about, either. He wasn't trying to do anything for himself.

He'd just wanted something so badly that he tried to make it into the truth. He'd probably believed it himself. He'd seen what

162

should have been the truth and what he wanted everything to be like. He'd tried to make the world better in a strange way—that was it. It was his way of changing things, kind of like writing fiction. That was different from lying or spinning. People who do those things don't have good intentions—that's the difference. They're different from people who want to make the world better and happier. Aren't they?

"I'm tired," Dad says. "Liza and Jane—can you clean up the kitchen? I'm going to bed."

He stops by Mom's chair and puts his head on hers. Mom reaches up and squeezes him around the neck. Then she smiles.

I look at Will and realize he's failing me. I can't believe it. I don't think he can, either. But we both know it. He's always taken care of me, made everything all right. And now he can't.

Everything I've always loved about him—his optimism, his high spirits, his buoyancy—all of that is what's failing me now. Everything I love about him is breaking my heart.

Why can't we talk about what's real—that I may be dying? I try, but he won't let me. He talks about not getting depressed, not giving up. He talks about the stem-cell transplant and how important it is to fight. He talks at me, through me, over me—but he never says a goddamn thing that's real and true. He never tells me how scared he is.

You can't run away from this. That's what I keep trying to tell him, but he doesn't hear me. Why can't we talk about our fears and nightmares together, drag them into the daylight? What would they look like then? Wouldn't it be better if we faced them together?

I don't know. God, I don't know. All I know is, I'm facing this and I'm all alone. When did this happen? When did I become the strong one?

The next morning, Ariel's picture is on the front page of the local newspaper. In it, she's standing in front of the school with her hands in the air, like she doesn't know what she's going to do next. It's right by a headline that says, *Houston High Honor Student Suspended for "Speaking Her Mind."* You can tell the reporter thinks that Mrs. Thomas has a screw loose. *Reached at her home for comment on the suspension, Mrs. Thomas refused to amplify her empirical basis for her logic about banning the color red or to say whether the ban had been successful,* the article says. Then it quotes several lines from the column Ariel wrote about students' getting sunburns or having red hair.

"Is this your friend—Ariel?" Dad asks, pointing at the article. "The one you're on the newspaper with?"

It's the first time he's asked me anything about school or myself in days. Maybe I shouldn't worry about his asking about driver's ed, either. Right now, Dad's so strange and preoccupied that he doesn't notice anything about Jane or me. I guess he thinks Granddad is looking out for us.

"We're not exactly friends." But I can tell Dad's not even listening to me. He asked me a question, then he forgot all about it.

I know he's thinking about Mom a lot right now. But why isn't he looking better, the way she is? I don't know. At least they aren't fighting the way they were the other night. So they must be getting along a lot better, even if they're not talking as much as they used to. So why can't he talk about any of it? He always said he wanted us to be closer as a family—especially because Mom was sick. After Mom's first diagnosis, he spent lots of time with Jane and me, talking to us and helping us plan how to make things better.

This time, he's not like that at all. He's entirely different. Right now, he doesn't know anything about me or what's going on in my life. He has no idea. I'm not sure he even cares.

I open the newspaper so I can read the rest of the article. At the very end, the reporter writes about Mr. Sorensen. *Journalism teacher Steve Sorensen, who has had primary responsibility for the school newspaper, said his recent resignation was unrelated to Ms. Lowenthal's controversial op-ed piece. "It was time for me to quit—that's all," Mr. Sorensen said. Mrs. Thomas said she could not comment on a personnel matter and was busy looking for another teacher who could assume Mr. Sorensen's responsibilities. "We wish him well in all his future endeavors," the principal said.*

I stare at the words. I can't believe what I'm seeing. *Recent resignation.* Mr. Sorensen had resigned. He'd resigned and he hadn't even said anything to me about it yesterday. He hadn't said a thing about himself. It was like it hadn't mattered to him at all. He was only trying to talk about me.

❧ ❧ ❧

When Dad drops me off in front of the high school, I get out and lean back in to tell him good-bye. He's staring straight ahead, like he doesn't know where he is. When I tell him good-bye, he almost jumps. For a few seconds, I could swear he almost doesn't recognize me.

He turns to face me. In the daylight, his face looks even worse—thinner and almost hollow. He's always been so handsome and looked so young for his age. But now he doesn't. He looks so old and sad and tired that it chills me.

There's something else, too, that I've never seen before. He looks helpless, that's it. *Helpless.* It doesn't belong on him. It doesn't fit, because that's not the kind of person he is. But it's there.

"Don't forget," he says, "you're taking your mother to the wig shop tomorrow morning." Then he drives off a lot faster than he should. He's probably late to work. He's late to everything these days. I wonder if he can even focus on his work right now. He always says how important the ability to concentrate is. But he doesn't look like he can concentrate on anything.

I've never seen Dad like this before. Up to now, there's never been anything he couldn't handle. He's an extraordinary person. That's what everybody's always said about him. That's what I've always thought, too. He always knows what to do. He's the strongest one in our family. If we can't depend on him, what are we going to do?

Everything's wrong. Every single thing in the world. I want to stretch out next to the side of the building and howl like a three-year-old because it hurts so much. Mr. Sorensen is leaving, and it's my fault. I flunked driver's ed, which is also my fault. Dad looks like he's seen a ghost, and I don't know whose fault that is. Nobody's acting the way they should. Everything's a complete mess. This isn't what my life is supposed to be like. I know that, damnit. I used to be happy and now all I want to do is to get away from everything and everybody.

"What's wrong?" Richard asks when I get to his locker. He's the only one who even notices there's something wrong. He gives me a soft kiss on my forehead, even though it's against school rules. Then he ruffles my hair. "I'm looking forward to tomorrow night," he says into my ear.

So am I. God, so am I. I smile up at Richard and look him straight in the eye and something wonderful washes over me. Just being with him, I'm feeling better already. I can hardly wait till tomorrow night. I don't know where Richard and I are going—and I don't care. What difference does it make, as long as it's far away? I just want to be with him and forget about everything that's going wrong with my whole screwed-up life. Right now, he's the only good thing I've got. The only thing that makes any sense.

When I come into French, Rory's bent over a novel. "Hi," I whisper across the aisle. "What's going on?"

She raises her eyebrows and shrugs, but doesn't say anything. I guess it must be a very interesting novel. Rory's always reading something. She might be close to flunking out of school, but she's extremely well-read. Her favorite character is Anna Karenina. I know that's the name of a novel, but I've never read it. So I just nodded when she told me about it. Since then, *Anna Karenina*'s been on my list of books to read, but I haven't gotten around to it yet. I've been too busy with lots of other things, I guess.

After class is over, I wave good-bye to Richard and try to catch up with Rory. She's a few feet ahead of me in the hall, walking fast. She must be dying for a cigarette.

"Rory! Hold on!" I pull at her elbow and her sweater falls off her shoulders. We both stoop to pick it up.

Rory's face is flushed. "Leave me alone, Liza. I don't want to be around anybody right now."

"What's wrong?"

Rory turns toward me and stops. "What do you mean, what's wrong? Don't you ever have a bad day, Liza? A really fucking-awful bad day when you think you should just put a gun to your head and get it over with because it hurts too much?"

Her eyes are bright green and glittery, and she stares at me like she wants to slap me. "Well, that's the kind of day I'm having," she says. "Understand?"

"Do you want to talk—" I reach out and touch her on the shoulder.

"No, I do not want to talk about it. Save the shrink shit for yourself, Liza. You need it more than I do."

Rory wrenches her shoulder away and glares at me. Then something happens to her face. It softens, and she looks like herself again. "Jesus," she says. "You look like hell, Liza. You look worse than I do. What's wrong with you, sweetie?"

Around us, students are rushing to get to class and the bell's ringing loudly. Rory grabs my arm. "Let's get out of this pit," she says.

We hurry out one of the side doors and head into the parking lot in front of the building. This is where the teachers park. The wind's whistling through the rows of cars, and I follow Rory while she walks from car to car, peering in. "Here's one," she says. She opens the door of a white Honda and slides in. Then she motions me to follow. I duck inside and close the door.

"Rory, whose car is this? I don't think—"

Rory's already fishing for the cigarettes in her purse. She waves a hand airily. "Somebody who's too goddamn dumb to lock their car. Serves 'em right for not being safety-conscious." She holds up a crumpled pack of cigarettes. "Want one?"

I say no, and she lights one and exhales. The whole car fills with smoke. Rory puts her head on the headrest and lifts her chin into the air. "I feel sorry for people who don't smoke," she says. Then she reaches over and pats me on the arm. "So talk to me, Liza darlin'. Tell me everything."

I talk. For a few minutes, I talk about everything. Mom's stem-cell transplant. The way she's acting around Dad. The fights they've been having. How terrible Dad looks. Mr. Sorensen's resignation. The wreck. Failing driver's ed. Everything.

For a few minutes, it feels better, just to let it all go and to stop trying so hard, pushing so much. For just a few minutes, the words pour out of me and up into the air, mingling with Rory's stale smoke, and I feel lighter—like I've finally managed to run faster than everything that's behind me. For just a few minutes.

Then I stop talking, and it all comes back. That unbearable weight that's been crushing me. I can feel my eyes fill with tears, but I know I can't let that happen. Not now. I've stopped for just a little while, and maybe that wasn't a good idea. I have to pick up everything and go on and be strong and positive. Because there's nobody else I can depend on. There's nobody but me.

I let out a breath and sigh. It's louder than I expected. I stare outside, through the winding fingers of smoke, and take a deep breath. A terrible pain is growing somewhere inside me. But I can't give in to it. I can't.

"So this is what smoking is like," I say in a lighter voice. I have to change the subject. I can't go on talking like this, feeling sorry for myself. It's time to get out of the car. I have to move on.

Rory's stuffing her cigarettes back into her purse. She doesn't say anything. For once, she's been completely quiet, just listening to me.

I hope she's not feeling sorry for me. I hate it when people do that. I hate the way they look at you, trying to find something in your face, the way Barbara did yesterday. I don't want anyone to look at me like that. I'm not the kind of person who needs pity. I'm not like that, at all. I hope Rory knows that.

We close the car doors as quietly as we can, and thread our way through the parking lot. Rory shakes out her hair. It's black today, and it blows in the wind like a skinny tumbleweed. Rory always feels like being a brunette in the winter, she says.

Before we go in the front door, we stop and look at each other. "Thanks for listening," I say. Then I try to stretch my mouth into a big smile, but it feels frozen. "I feel a lot better now, Rory. I know everything's going to be okay. I can feel it."

Rory's still quiet, squinting at me. The sun's come out, and it's one of those bright, beautiful winter days we always have in Austin. That's good. Isn't it? That's a good sign. Yes, it is. It has to be.

I lift my face up into the sunlight, but it's still cold out here. All I can feel is the wind.

"Everything is going to be fine," I say. "I know it is."

Rory doesn't say a word. Her eyes are on the sidewalk. Then she shakes her head, just barely.

❧ ❧ ❧

"Why aren't you wearing red, Liza?" Mr. Sorensen asks.

The last bell's just rung, and I'm sitting in the journalism room. I'm the only one here, aside from him. I need to go through the letters I've gotten this week.

"What?"

Mr. Sorensen is pacing around the room. He stops and points to his red plaid shirt.

Oh, that's right. Half the student body wore red today. But nothing happened, because Mrs. Thomas got on the intercom before lunch and announced that the ban on red was over. It had already been a great success, she said, and there was no reason to continue it. It was a smart thing to do. It made me think Mrs. Thomas isn't as dumb as Ariel thinks she is.

"I guess I forgot about it," I say.

Mr. Sorensen walks back to his desk. He has two large cardboard boxes on it, and he's packing things into them.

Today is his last day. He told our class he didn't want a party or for anyone to make a big deal out of it. So we didn't. We just sat and listened to him talk about how much he'd loved teaching us—but it was time for him to leave. We were all so surprised by how fast everything's happened that no one could say anything.

"It's funny how much stuff you accumulate," he's saying right now, "even when you don't think you're going to be staying in a place. I've been here six years—a lot longer than I ever thought I would."

"Mr. Sorensen—did you really resign? Or did Mrs. Thomas—"

He shakes his head. "I really resigned, Liza. Mrs. Thomas didn't have the chance to fire me."

"But you can't quit just because of this. You're a wonderful teacher. I—"

He interrupts me. "I'm not quitting because of this, Liza. I'm quitting for lots of reasons. I hadn't realized how unhappy I was—till this happened." He unloads a stack of papers into one of the boxes and smiles at me. It's a sad, tired smile. "So, you see—Ariel may have done me a strange kind of favor. Someday, I'll have to thank her for it."

Why is he acting like he didn't have any choices? Why is he just giving in? How can he give up like that—without fighting? Why is he leaving us?

"But—but she couldn't have fired you. You could have fought it, Mr. Sorensen. We could have all fought it. We would have helped you. You know that."

He shakes his head again, impatiently. "You're not listening to what I'm saying, Liza."

"But you're giving up. You should never—"

For the first time, Mr. Sorensen looks angry. "I am not giving up, Liza. Listen to what I'm saying. I'm not fighting—because it isn't worth it to me. I don't want it. I don't want what you want. I want—well, I don't know what I want. But not this." He closes the box and tapes it shut. "I don't want to stay here."

"But that's not right, Mr. Sorensen." My voice is high and squeaky. I sound like I'm three years old or something, and I've gotten lost in a department store. That's the way I feel, all of a sudden—like everything around me is so enormous and I need somebody bigger who can help me get out. I can't do this by myself. Not any longer. I thought I could. But I was wrong.

Mr. Sorensen sits down in his chair and sighs. "It isn't a matter of right and wrong, Liza. Can't you see that? This isn't what I want—and you can't make me want it. I don't want this fight. I don't want this job. I'm unhappy here. There are lots of other things I care about more."

He stands up and lifts the box off his desk. "I'm going to pack this in my car." His voice is flat. He's telling me we're at the end of our conversation.

❊❊❊   ❊❊❊   ❊❊❊

For the next hour, I sit at my desk and read letters. Mr. Sorensen goes on packing his boxes and taking them back and forth to his car. He hasn't said anything about Mom or how I didn't want to talk about her. We're not saying anything to each other.

I look back at the letter in my hand. I've already read it two or three times, and I don't know why I'm doing it again.

Dear Deborah, My stepfather calls me a whore and tells me to get out of the house if I don't like it. . . . Dear Deborah—My family's on food stamps right now. I hate it when we go to the grocery store. . . . Dear Deborah, What makes you think you know everything? I bet you're as dumb as the rest of us. Your real name isn't even Deborah, is it? . . . Dear Deborah, My dog died last week. . . . Dear Deborah: What's the best way to kill yourself? My friend says if you shoot yourself in the temple . . .

These letters are awful. I can't help these people. What do I know about anything? What kind of difference can I make?

I try to focus. I have to focus. I answer the first three letters. I just sit there and blast them out on the computer. I'm not even sure what I'm saying. But now I've been doing this for so long that I'm pretty good at coming up with the same formula. *See a counselor.* . . . *Remember, everybody has problems.* . . . *Things will get better.* . . . *Don't give up.* . . . *You have to look on the positive side of things.* . . . *This will make you stronger.* . . . *You won't believe this, but* . . .

I hit the Send button hard. I'm finished. I've come up with every corny bit of advice I can. They'll print the letters and answers in the newspaper, and maybe it will help someone. Who knows? Who in the hell knows?

The answers are easy for me. They're what I've been saying all my life. They're everything that Dad's taught me. They're true. They're right. I believe in them.

But now they're making me feel emptier and sadder than I've ever felt in my life. They used to seem almost magical because they were so powerful and true. But they don't feel like anything now. They're just a bunch of dead, empty words. Right now, I feel like I do when Dad talks to me these days—like he doesn't believe what he's saying any longer, and neither do I. What we're saying isn't enough. We're trying to act like we're the same people we used to be, but we're not. We're different. Everything we used to do doesn't work any longer.

When did this happen? When is it going to stop? When is it all going to be over?

I can't stay here. I've got to go. I don't know where I'm going, but I have to hurry. Maybe, if I jog a long, long time, I'll feel better.

I pull my backpack on and get up to leave. Mr. Sorensen

looks up. He's still packing boxes and mopping his face. It's hot in here.

"Mr. Sorensen . . . I'll really miss you. I'm sorry that . . . everything happened. I'm really sorry."

He's sitting right underneath the portrait of Deborah Ames. Their expressions are the same, I notice—like they're sadder than anybody else and they know more. Like they know too much they don't want to know.

"You've been a wonderful student, Liza. I've enjoyed knowing you. I mean that."

"Can I ask you—well, where you're going? Are you going to be all right?"

"I don't know where I'm going, Liza. But I'm going to be all right." He pauses for just a second.

"What about you, Liza?" he asks. "Are *you* going to be all right?"

❦ ❦ ❦

The next morning, I drive Mom to the wig store as slowly as possible. I don't want to do anything wrong. The Driving Safe-T people might have notified the police that I'm a dangerous driver. They might have orders to arrest me on sight.

Mom presses the button on the door and opens her window. "It's nice to be out. I always feel so much better when I get out of the house." The wind ruffles her hair. Before she got chemo the last time, she had straight hair, but it's grown back curly. That happens a lot. They call it "chemo curl."

I can remember how excited she was the first time she took off her wig in August. Her hair was really, really short, but it looked good on her. "It's because you have such great cheekbones, Becca," Dad told her. "You look beautiful." And she did. She looked beautiful and happy. That seems so long ago, like something that happened in a movie or something that happened to someone else. I can't believe it was just a few months ago.

I don't want to think about Mom's hair right now, and how it's going to fall out again. I can't. It won't do any good. We need to concentrate on finding the most glamorous wig we can. That will help. It will make Mom feel a lot better about her stem-cell transplant.

I pull the car into the parking lot and slide it between two Suburbans. Naturally, I get too close to the one on the right, and Mom can't open her door. I've never been very good at parking. Mr. Bridges didn't teach me a thing about it, either.

So I finally pull out and go to the far side of the parking lot. I'm kind of on a yellow line, but I don't think that matters too much.

The wig store's called Special Needs by Geraldine. It's the same place Mom went last year with another friend of hers. I guess they gave it a name like that so people wouldn't get it confused with regular wig places. It's only for women who've gone bald. Most of them are going through chemo, but Dad says there are other diseases that can make you go bald, too.

There's a woman behind the counter. She must be Geraldine. She's tall and thin, and she has on a platinum blond wig. She's also wearing enough makeup for every girl in our sophomore class.

"Oh, hon." Geraldine comes out from behind the counter and she takes Mom's hand. "I hope this is just a social visit—just t'see how I'm doing."

She looks at Mom, and Mom doesn't say anything. Geraldine moves closer and hugs her. They stand like that for a long time, without moving at all. When they finally pull apart, they both wipe their eyes. Geraldine has a long streak of black mascara running down her cheek. She's still holding Mom's hand.

"We'll get you fixed up, hon," Geraldine says. "The best way we know how."

Mom sits in a revolving chair in front of a three-way mirror. It's just like a hairdresser's place. Geraldine brushes Mom's hair back and pins it up. "Came back pretty, didn't it?" She leans over and puts her face next to Mom's. "What d'you want this time, hon?"

"I don't know." Mom shakes her head. "What do you think, Liza?" It's the first thing anybody's said to me since we came in the store. Mom hasn't even introduced me to Geraldine, which is strange. She's always telling us how important good manners are.

"This is my older daughter, Liza," Mom says to Geraldine.

"You look just like your mama, hon," Geraldine says. "I would've known you anywhere."

That's funny. No one's ever said that to me before. Everyone always says I look just like Dad. I smile at Geraldine's reflection in the mirror and wonder what she's seeing.

Mom and Geraldine sit and talk while I walk around the store and stare at all the wigs on the shelves around us. I've never picked out new hair before, and I don't know what to do. The wigs are on white Styrofoam heads—red, blond, black, and gray wigs, short and medium-length, long and really long, curly and straight. If you look really closely, you can see the heads have faces with small smiles on them.

I try to imagine Mom wearing one of those wigs—that short, ash-blond one that curls into soft ringlets around the face. How would it look? I don't know. I've never been that good at visualizing things. I'm not a very artistic person, like Mom is.

I squint my eyes and try to concentrate. I try to see what Mom would look like, wearing that hair. It's hard to focus, so I grit my teeth and close my eyes and concentrate harder. For a few seconds, everything turns black. Then, out of nowhere, some kind of vision smashes into me, like I can see a bigger, brighter world with my eyes shut. I can see the wig and I can tell Mom's wearing it—but her face is blank and white and still, like the Styrofoam heads. Her eyes are closed. She can't move. She can't talk, she can't breathe. Her face is a mask, and she's left it behind. She's gone somewhere far away. The mask is all we have left.

Oh, my God. I'm going to be sick. I know I'm going to be sick. I'm bending over, nauseated, clutching my stomach, and I'm shivering. I keep trying to catch my breath, but I can't. I can't breathe. I can't breathe at all, because I'm crying too hard.

"Goddamnit. Goddamnit to fucking hell." I can hear someone saying that over and over, screaming. I could swear it's my voice, except I never say things like that. I never scream.

"It's all right, Lizzie. Oh, babe, it's all right. Come here."

All of a sudden, I'm sitting on Mom's lap, and she has her arms around me. I don't know where Geraldine has gone. It's just Mom and me, swaying back and forth in that revolving chair with the green seat. We sit there for a long, long time, surrounded by all the mirrors and lights and wigs and white heads that stare at us and smile.

❧ ❧ ❧

Mom and I drive home. We don't talk much. I feel so exhausted, I can hardly move. That's why Mom's driving. Or maybe it's because she thinks I'm going crazy. Maybe that's it. She doesn't trust me to drive any longer. When she thinks I don't notice, she looks at me out of the corner of her eye. That's exactly the way people look at you when they think you're crazy.

177

We pull into the garage, and for a few minutes, we just sit there. All I can hear is the sounds the car makes while it winds down and turns off. Then it's quiet. Mom swallows. I can even hear that.

"Liza . . . we've got to talk," she says.

Talk. We've got to talk. I hate it when people say things like that. You always know you're going to hear something terrible when someone says you have to talk. I don't want to talk. I don't want to listen, either. I want to get out of the car and run away, before it's too late. I'm fast. I could run forever. I could leave all of this behind. I could be happy again.

"We haven't been talking about what's going on with us . . . and with me." Mom doesn't look at me. She's staring at her hands on the steering wheel. They're still clutching the wheel like she's driving. "Your father hasn't wanted to tell you and Jane how serious this is—how sick I am. He didn't want to tell you—and he didn't want to know, himself. I thought he was right, at first. But now, I don't."

Mom turns to me. "Babe . . . I told you everything's going to be all right . . . and it will be, somehow. I don't know how, but it will be."

She puts my left hand between her two hands and rubs it softly. "But I may not get well . . . and that's something I want us to face, instead of ignoring. I want us to open our eyes. I want to see what's really there . . . no matter how much it hurts."

Mom pauses and sighs. "Can you understand what I'm saying, Liza? I know you don't want to face this. You don't want it, and your father doesn't, either. But it's the only way I know how to live right now. It's a decision I have to make—how I'm going to live the rest of my life."

What's she trying to tell me? My heart's beating loud and fast, and I think I'm having one of those panic attacks. I feel terrible.

"Mom—does that mean you're not going through with the

178

stem-cell transplant?" She doesn't answer, and I rush on. "You're trying to run away from your illness—and you can't. You can't run away from it."

"I'm not running away from it, Liza. That's what everyone else is doing—can't you see that? But I can't—"

"But you're giving up, Mom. You're—"

Mom takes my shoulders in her hands and gives me a little shake. "Look at me, Liza," she says. "Look me in the eyes." Her eyes are wet, but they're clear and strong, that same deep blue they've always been. "I'm *not* giving up, Liza. Stop saying that. I'm trying to accept something I have to accept. Don't you see the diff—"

The light in the garage goes on. Dad's standing there in the doorway. He walks to Mom's side and opens the door. "My God, Rebecca—where have you been?" he says. He looks like he's angry and scared at the same time. "You've got a doctor's appointment in five minutes. Did you forget?"

Mom yanks off her seat belt and gets out of the car. "No, I did not, Will. I didn't forget a damned thing—and I never have. You drive. We can be late. That fucking oncologist can wait. He's kept me waiting enough times." She slams the door. "Wait here. I'll be right back."

Dad opens the door again and slides into the driver's seat, next to me. "Good fucking God, Liza. Why in the bloody hell didn't you tell me what happened in driver's ed? The school called this morning—and I didn't know a thing, because you hadn't told me. What happened? You had a wreck and you forgot to tell me?"

I've never seen Dad this angry before. His face is so red it's almost purple.

"I didn't want to worry you," I say. "You seemed—"

"Didn't want to worry me?" Dad's voice is so different, I almost don't recognize it. It's ugly and mean. Where is that voice coming

179

from? It can't be him. It isn't him. "With everything that's going on with your mother—you go and have a wreck and you didn't want to worry me? What in the hell is wrong with you, anyway?"

My car door opens and Mom's standing there. I don't know what she's heard. She kisses me on the forehead when I get out of the car, then she gets in. For just a minute, Dad stares at me, still looking furious. Then something happens to his face. It almost seems to melt. He looks like he's going to cry, all of a sudden, like he wants to put his head on the steering wheel and scream and cry. But that's impossible. It's something I've never seen before. I can't be seeing it now.

I walk inside and listen to them back slowly into the street. The tires screech when Dad puts the car into gear.

❦ ❦ ❦

I brush my hair back and stare at myself in the mirror. My eyes look different than they usually do—almost wild, like they want to tear themselves out of my face. My face doesn't look the same, either. It's like somebody else's face, somebody who's unhappy and tortured and crazy and unpredictable. I don't know who's staring back at me, but I don't want to see her anymore.

I turn off the light in my bathroom, where I'm standing. It's almost dark, and I can't see the face now. I can only see a silhouette in front of me, a shadowy figure in front of the gray wall. It feels better to stand in the shadows where I don't have to see things I don't want to see. I don't want to see anything right now, especially myself.

Richard's going to be here soon. I need to get dressed and put some makeup on. Maybe that will help. Maybe I'll look more normal that way. I can't see my old face, so maybe I can draw it on myself.

Downstairs, a door slams. I can hear people yelling at each other, and I know it must be Mom and Dad. I can tell they're angry, but I can't understand what they're saying. They're too far away.

I open my door quietly. I don't know what they're saying—but I can't stop myself, either. For some reason, it makes me think of the time we passed a horrible wreck on the highway on the way to Dallas. There was a smashed car on the median and a woman was inside it. I turned around and watched till the twisted car got smaller and smaller and I couldn't see it any longer.

That's what I feel now. I can't stand to hear what Mom and Dad are saying. It's terrible for me when they fight—like they're ripping apart pieces of my heart. But I have to get closer. My heart's getting ripped apart anyway, by the sound of their voices. Maybe the words won't make that much difference. But I have to hear them.

I lean over the railing and close my eyes so I can hear better. I hear a sound I've never heard before, of someone crying. It's low and brokenhearted, almost like an animal that's been hurt. It's a voice I've never heard before, but I know it belongs to Dad.

"Don't do this," he's saying. "You . . . can't . . . you can't . . ."

His voice gets lower so that it's almost a soft, low rumble, and I can't understand what he's saying. I can only understand the tone of his voice—almost like it's a color I can see, black and harsh and hopeless. Mom's voice is higher-pitched and pleading, lighter-colored, firmer somehow. I listen to the voices crash into each other for a few minutes, then they stop. The only sound I can hear is of someone crying. It's Dad again. I know it's Dad.

This isn't right. Dad never cries. It's Mom, always Mom. She's the one who gives up and needs the rest of us to help her. Is that what's happening now? She's given up and she's scared and depressed and Dad can't talk her into fighting and living? Is that what he's crying about? Does he need me to help him now? Maybe it's all been too much for him.

I slide down the stairs, trying not to make any noise. The low murmur of voices from the kitchen gets clearer.

"I can't live the way you want me to, Will. I can't do it. I've tried all my life, and I have to stop. Can't you understand that? Can't you understand that the time comes when it's all right to let go? When you need to stop struggling so much? Can't you understand that—goddamnit to hell?

"Can you let me do that? Will you? Because that's what I'm going to do—whether you want it or not. I'm going to let somebody else fight this—not me. I want to live. That's—"

The doorbell rings and the voices stop. It must be Richard. I slip back up the stairs, panting, with my heart beating hard and fast. I pull some clothes from my closet and put them on in the dark. I don't care what I'm wearing. I don't care what I look like. What does it matter what you look like, anyway, when your heart is breaking?

I close the door to my room and look across the landing. Jane's sitting there, with her legs crossed and her head in her hands. Her hair's spilling onto the floor, tangled and snarled, like she hasn't combed it in days. She must have been there all the time.

❧ ❧ ❧

"What do you want to do tonight?" Richard says.

It's a cool night, but we've got the windows rolled down in Richard's car. The air rushes in and soothes my face. It catches my hair and makes it fly behind me.

Fly—that's what I'd like to do tonight. I want to soar into the sky, where everything is dark and sparkly and find new places and never come back. I'll just keep moving. I'll never stop. I'll just go farther and farther away and pretty soon, I'll forget what I left behind. I want to forget everything. I don't want to be where I am right now. I used to like where I was. Now I hate it. I don't belong here. Everything's changed and it doesn't make sense to me. I need to go away.

"Your parents weren't bad at all," Richard says. "I liked them. They seemed a little upset about something, though."

He reaches over and puts his hand on my neck. It feels incredibly good and warm. Maybe, if I'm going away, I should take Richard with me. He's the only person I like these days. Everybody else can leave me alone and go straight to hell.

"What do you want to do?" he asks again.

"I'm not sure." I run my fingers along his right forearm. The hair on his arm is silky and warm, and it feels good to touch it. "We could go away to Mexico. It's not that far away."

He laughs, like I'm joking. Then he glances at me. "You seem strange tonight, Liza. Are you okay?"

"I'm fine." I run my fingers up his arm. He has a blue cotton shirt on, with the sleeves rolled up to his elbow. The material feels smooth and soft. "I just feel like doing something—I don't know—*different* for a change. What's wrong with that? Why do I have to act like the same boring person all the time? I'm sick of being such a good girl." I throw my head back on the car seat. "I want to fly tonight."

Richard shifts gears and smiles at me again. "I think we can arrange that," he says.

Will cried tonight, making sounds I'd never heard him make before. Once, those sounds would have broken my heart. Today, I know that I can bear them. I can take care of him for a while.

183

I have to be the one who carries us, just for now. I realized that when Liza began to scream and cry today. I held her for so long in my lap, comforting her, for the first time in years. She was like a small child.

Sitting there, I was overwhelmed by my feelings for her and Jane. God, there's something so primitive and gut-wrenching and fierce about that love. I would do anything to protect them and take care of them as long as I can. Anything. I'd throw myself in front of a speeding car, if that would help. Or kill anyone who hurt them. I'd do anything for them, legal or illegal, moral or immoral. It wouldn't matter to me. I'd do it without thinking.

I don't know where these feelings came from. But I know I don't own them. They own me.

Finally, after all of this time, I understand something. I will not survive this. But that love will, always.

We're sitting at the top of Mount Bonnell, one of the tallest hills in Austin. You can see the state capitol from here and the UT Tower and all the buildings downtown. Below us, Lake Austin is dark and quiet, and there are bright white lights from all the houses on the other side of the water. We're surrounded by all that dark and those white lights, high up in the air, just like I wanted. The wind blows through my hair, and I feel lighter and happier than I have in a long, long time.

"Try this," Richard says. He hands me a plastic glass filled with 7UP and some kind of liquor, then he pours himself one. We went by his house to pick up the liquor, since his father is out of town. Richard says his father doesn't care if he drinks, as long as he's responsible about it. My parents always said they wanted me to talk to them when I was tempted to drink. I said I would. But I can't talk to them right now. Not about drinking or anything else. They don't have time to think about my problems these days.

"Cheers," Richard says. We touch our plastic glasses together. I've drunk a little champagne a few times, but this is the first hard liquor I've ever tried. It tastes awful, kind of like gasoline. But I make myself sip it slowly and think about something else. It's an acquired taste, just like coffee. That's what I've always heard. Tonight, I'm going to acquire it.

Richard puts his arm around me and leans his head against mine. We're sitting on a blanket he brought from his car. Mount Bonnell's empty tonight, and we're the only people here. I guess it's because it's still a little cold outside. If it weren't for all those lights around us, I'd think we were the only people on earth. Everything else seems so far away.

I take a larger sip of my drink, and notice it doesn't taste as bad as it did at first. I can feel it inside me, making me relaxed and carefree and happy. *Carefree.* I've never felt like that in my life.

We sit together, drinking and watching the night spread out in front of us. We don't talk. We just drink and breathe and sometimes one of us sighs. We're so close that it feels like we're breathing at the same time. I've never felt this close to anyone before. I smile at Richard and smooth his hair back from his forehead. His face is soft and warm against my fingers. I sigh again. Maybe I'm the only one who's doing the sighing.

I drink some more, holding my glass carefully. Every time I take another swig, I can feel my body soften. What a wonderful feeling, just like I'm floating.

"I think I like drinking," I say. "I am very . . . *impressed* with it."

Richard and I laugh when I say that, like it's a very funny thing to say. I don't know why it's funny. But the truth is, it's hilarious. I throw my head back and laugh, like I'm talking to the sky and it's going to answer me back. That's such a funny idea that I laugh even more. I can almost see my laughter rushing off the top of the mountain, winding its way into the galaxy, spilling and breaking and looping into the dark, dark sky. It's a beautiful picture. Beautiful. Right now, everything's beautiful. It's so beautiful and gorgeous and spectacular and thrilling and fun that I want to laugh and cry and scream at the same time.

"We've got more where that came from." Richard pulls the soft-drink can and liquor bottle out of a paper sack and pours more for both of us. His arm jolts a little and liquid foams over the tops of the cups and spills on the blanket.

"Our cups runneth over, so we should runneth to our cups," he says. "That comes from the Bible, I think." He touches my glass with his again. "Bottoms up. That *doesn't* come from the Bible."

I nod. "That's all right. I think the Bible is a highly . . . *overrated* book." I splash the drink into my mouth, and it warms me as it goes down. My mouth is working very, very slowly, like it's bigger and heavier than it used to be. I need to *e-nun-ci-ate* more clearly. "I mean—just because God wrote it, everybody thinks it's so great.

"You know what I think?" It's a good thing I'm talking slowly, since my mind feels like it's made of molasses. "I think the Holy Spirit must be God's ghostwriter. It's very clear to me now. Will you write that down for me, Richard? I think it's . . . a very important . . . theological point. I don't want to forget it."

"I'll write it down later," Richard says. He turns and looks at me. His eyes are reflecting some of the lights. They're velvety and beautiful, just like the sky. He takes the drink out of my hand. The cup's almost empty.

Then he turns my face to his and kisses me. His mouth is soft and moist, and all I want to do is get closer and closer to him and be with him like this and never move again. He strokes my hair and kisses my neck, and I pull him toward me. It's just like I thought. We're the only two people on earth. There's nothing outside of us. We're in the middle of some kind of crazy, spinning, powerful storm of darkness and light and cool winds.

"I love you," he whispers in my ear. His voice is soft and low and husky. "God, you're the most beautiful thing I've ever seen, Liza. I thought that the first time I saw you."

We stretch out our legs and lie on the blanket. I can feel his body giving me warmth, making me feel light and ecstatic and buoyant. We're being absorbed by the sky and the stars and all the damp grass and rough wool and warm, soft skin. We're flinging ourselves into the universe, carried by some kind of strong, unyielding current. We're flying and laughing. We've escaped somewhere far, far away, and no one can find us. We're never coming back.

❧❧❧ ❧❧❧ ❧❧❧

Someone is kicking me in the head. It's a terrible, violent thing to do. I pull something soft over my head to protect it. But the kicking goes on and on, getting harder. I can't ignore it any longer. I have to stop it.

I yank my head up and look around. I'm in my own bedroom, and the sun is coming in through the slats of the shutters like jagged, white-yellow daggers. I pull the covers and pillow back over my head. I feel terrible. My mouth is dry and my head's throbbing and I'm pretty sure I'm about to throw up. I must have caught some terrible disease. I wonder if I'm dying.

I try to get up to go to the bathroom, then I sit right down on the floor. The room is moving. How can I walk if the room is moving? I can't. So I crawl along the floor very, very slowly till I get to the bathroom. I feel like a worm, inching along the carpet.

Finally, my hands hit the tiles on my bathroom floor, and I pull myself inside. I glide over the tiles to the toilet. I'm extremely happy to see the toilet. I've never realized how much I liked it before. From the floor, it looks like a ten-story building. I grab on to the seat and pull myself up.

I don't know how long I stay there, vomiting and wiping my face off with toilet paper, and vomiting again. When it's over, I lie back on the cool tiles and pull a bath towel over me so I won't be cold. I curl up and rub my arms and try to stay warm. I think I've finished vomiting. My stomach feels empty and shrunken. I wish my bed weren't so far away. It would be nice to lie on something soft and warm, instead of the cold floor.

I still can't walk. I'm too sick and dizzy. So I crawl back to my bed very slowly. I don't want to make sudden, jerky movements. I know that. I need to move very, very slowly, very, very smoothly. I reach my bed, finally, and push myself up as hard as I can. I roll into the bed and pull the covers back over my face and start to breathe more slowly. I still feel terrible, but at least I'm not sick to my stomach.

It must be two or three hours later when I wake up. The clock next to my bed is blurry, so I squint my eyes to focus better. Ten-thirty. I never sleep that late. I always have too many things to get done, like jogging. I don't think I'm going to jog this morning. I feel terrible. I'm lucky that I didn't die in my sleep.

I start an inventory from my head to my feet. Head fuzzy. Someone is still kicking it. My throat is dry and my mouth is drier and my whole body aches. This may be some new, terrible version of the flu.

Except. *Except.* Something's coming over me, and I realize I haven't been thinking straight. I've heard of people having symptoms like this, and I know what it must be. It isn't the flu. I've got a hangover. A hangover! I've never had a hangover before! I've answered two or three letters telling people how to deal with a hangover and never drink again. I thought it was kind of funny. But it's not. I'll never laugh at people with hangovers again.

What did I tell them? I had to ask Dad about it. Drink plenty of fluids. Take something for your headache. Sleep. Eat something, if you can.

I slide out of bed and stand up. Fortunately, the room's stopped moving and I can walk. I grab the glass in my bathroom and drink three or four cups of water. Then I peer into the mirror. My hair's like a tumbleweed, all snarled and electric, and my eyes are red and narrow. Mascara's streaked down my left cheek like a slash mark. I look like I'm about six hundred years old, one of those people who's been drinking for years and never stopped. A before ad for Alcoholics Anonymous.

I pull out a brush and untangle my hair. When I toss it back, I see a dark red mark on the side of my neck. It's just like the hangover news—I know about things like this because I've written about them and given other kids advice. This is a hickey on my neck. Good God. A hickey. That must mean that Richard and I—

All of a sudden, I feel like I've been hit by an avalanche. Richard and I—*what*? What happened? What did we do?

I sit down on the bathroom floor and try to think. I remember the cold night and all the stars and the view from Mount Bonnell and how beautiful everything was. I remember drinking more than I'd ever drunk in my life, and feeling happy and light, like I could float up into the sky.

I remember how Richard kissed me again and again, and how I pulled him on top of me and stroked his hair and his chest and felt deliriously happy and warm, like I didn't have any control over anything—and I didn't care anymore. I'd slipped out of myself, somehow, and someone else had come in, and I couldn't remember exactly what she'd done.

My stomach clenches again and my heart's pounding like a bass drum at a football game. I feel sick, even though I know I don't have anything more to vomit. There are sirens going off in my head and body, like wild, loud, shrieking birds.

My God, my God, my God, I think over and over. *My God, what happened? What did I do? Why can't I remember anything?*

❧❧❧ ❧❧❧ ❧❧❧

It's late afternoon before I finally stumble downstairs. I took a long, hot shower and didn't want to leave all that steam and warmth. I soaped my body again and again so I wouldn't feel so dirty and smell like vomit. I soaped my breasts, even though I didn't want to look at them. I could remember Richard touching them last night and how good it felt. It made me nauseated, just thinking about how good I'd felt.

Breasts are dangerous. Sex is dangerous. Love is even worse. Why didn't I know that? How could I have been such an idiot? What was wrong with me?

The house is quiet. There's nobody in the kitchen or living room. Even Granddad must have gone somewhere. I wonder where everybody is. I wonder why nobody noticed that I didn't get up this morning.

I pour myself a giant glass of orange juice and sip it at the kitchen counter. I'm glad there's nobody here to see how weird I look and how strange I'm acting. Every time I hear a noise, I jump. I know I still look awful, too, even though I cleaned off my face and

190

washed my hair. Anybody who looks at me can probably tell that something happened to me last night. They'll look at me and they'll know. They'll know everything just by looking at me.

So why don't *I* know?

I don't even know how I got home. I don't know when I got home, either. My usual curfew is midnight. Usually, Dad and Mom are still up when I come home from a date. Were they awake when I got back last night?

The door from the garage bangs shut, and Mom comes into the kitchen. She's dressed in a light-blue sweatsuit and a small cloud of L'Air du Temps. She puts her hand on my forehead. "Are you feeling better, babe?" she asks. "We tried to be quiet so you could sleep this morning."

What's she talking about? Does she know what happened? I search Mom's face for a few seconds. She looks concerned, that's all I can see. And sad and calm and something else I can't quite make out. But she looks different. For the first time in weeks, she doesn't look angry and distracted. Is that it? Is that what's different? She looks almost—*what*? Peaceful?

"I'm not feeling too well," I say as vaguely as I can. "I guess it was one of those . . . twenty-four-hour viruses."

"That's what Richard's note said. Your father and I had gone out driving and talking last night—and we didn't get back till after midnight. Richard left us a note in the kitchen about how you'd gotten sick and he'd brought you home and taken you upstairs. It was such a thoughtful thing for him to—"

The phone rings, and Mom answers it. "Yes, Richard. Good afternoon. Yes. She's sitting right here. I don't think she's completely recovered yet."

She hands me the phone and smiles.

"Hello?" It's the only thing I can say, with Mom standing right here, staring at me with a funny smile on her face. Hello! What do I mean, *hello*? I want to say, What happened last night? How did I get home? What did I do before I got home? What did we do? Tell me everything, you no-good, piece-of-shit bastard.

"Liza—you feeling better?"

Who does he think he is—calling up and asking me that, right in front of my mother? He's probably given me a venereal disease or something. Herpes, I bet. I've written lots of advice columns about guys like him. They're scum.

"Yes, thank you. I feel fine."

"You've never had anything to drink before, have you?" He sounds amused. What a jerk! He probably raped me! I should hang up right now and call the police. "I didn't realize you were in such bad shape till you passed out. That scared me to death. I had to practically carry you down the mountain." He chuckles. *Chuckles!* "You're a lot heavier than you look."

What does he mean by that? Does he think I'm fat or something? I don't say a word. I don't even breathe. People like him don't deserve to be talked to at all.

"Look," he says. "I was really worried about you—and I didn't want to get you in trouble with your parents, either."

I don't say anything, so he goes on. "We were lucky, though. They weren't there when we got to your house. That was really fortunate. You smelled like a brewery, and you could hardly stand up. I just took you upstairs and left a note for them. Was that okay? I didn't know what else to do."

"It was very considerate of you," I say in my iciest voice.

Mom glances at me and leaves the room. *Finally.* The minute the door swings shut, I lean into the phone and whisper. "Will you tell me what else happened last night? I can only remember the kissing and petting. What else happened?"

"What do you mean?" He sounds genuinely confused. He must lie all the time. Born liars get even better when they practice a lot. "Nothing else happened. We kissed for a while and then you passed out. So I took you home."

He pauses and his voice gets a little higher. "What do you think I did, Liza? Took advantage of you while you were passed out?"

I don't answer. His question lingers, echoing over and over. I can hear Richard breathing at the other end of the line.

"I can't believe it," he says after a few seconds. "Did you really think I'd do something like that?"

I draw my breath in, slowly. Could Richard be telling the truth? He didn't do anything. We didn't do anything. I just got drunk and passed out and he brought me home. Like he said, that was all that happened. Could that really be the truth?

Would he be calling me if it weren't the truth? I can see Richard's face at the other end of the line—how soft his eyes are and how there's something so sweet and whole and open about him that I like so much. How he told me he loved me. I can hear how he said it last night, with some kind of emotion in his voice I'd never heard anyone use before. I know boys tell girls they love them all the time, and lots of times, they don't mean it. But I don't think Richard was doing that. He's not like that. He's not that kind of person.

My head's starting to pound again. It hurts even worse than it did before.

"Is that what you're saying, Liza? Do you really think I—"

"No . . . no. Of course I don't think that, Richard." I say that before I think it. But something about it seems right. "I know you wouldn't do anything like that. I know you . . . too well."

Richard doesn't say anything.

I draw a deep breath and try to think. "Richard, I didn't know—I mean, I'm sorry. You're right. I'd never drunk anything before. I just went out of my mind. I couldn't remember anything . . . and it scared me. It scared me to death."

There's still silence at his end of the line. But he hasn't hung up on me.

"Richard, please forgive me. Please. You don't understand a lot of things—you don't understand because I haven't told you anything." I lean back from the phone and rest my head so that I'm staring up at the ceiling. "I just have so many . . . so many awful things going on right now. My mother's sick and my journalism teacher quit and I just had a wreck . . . and I feel like I'm fucking up everything in my life . . . and I don't know why. I don't understand anything in my life right now. And now I've done this, and I feel terrible . . . because I like you so much. And I wanted you to like me."

I hear Richard draw a breath at the other end of the line. But he doesn't say anything.

"Richard?"

"I'm here." His voice is heavy, like he's just realized he's tired. But at least he's still talking to me.

❦ ❦ ❦

"My God. You sound terrible, Liza. Are you sick?" It's Rory. She's not even bothering to say hello today. "I call you up to hear about your fabulous date—and you sound like death on wheels." She inhales a cigarette at the other end of the line. "What gives? Did he stand you up or something?"

"No." I'm lying on my bed, trying to meditate so my head will stop throbbing. So far, it's not working.

Rory would think it's hilarious if she knew what a bad hangover I have. That's why I'm not going to tell her.

194

"What do you mean—*no*? Is that all you have to say? You sound horrible. What happened?"

"It isn't Richard." When I say that, the same thing happens again. I say it without thinking and, the minute I hear it, I realize it's true. I like Richard better than any boy I've ever dated, and I'm sorry I hurt his feelings. I hope we'll see each other again.

But he's not the reason I feel so bad—like my heart is breaking. It's every other thing in my life that I've always depended on. My parents. Myself. Everything that's happened to me at school and in driver's ed. It's all part of the same thing. It's everything my life used to be—how I could understand it and control it and make sense out of it. It's everything I used to have, but don't have any longer. I don't know what I have. I don't know who I am, except I'm not the person I thought I was.

Right now, I'm not even sorry I have a hangover. I'd rather think about how much my head hurts—I'd rather think about anything on earth—than what's going on in my life. I'd rather spend the rest of my life lying on the bathroom floor if I didn't have to think about Dad's crying last night and what it must mean. Maybe that's why people drink. I've never understood it before— but maybe that's it. Anything's better than hurting this much. Anything.

"It isn't Richard," I say again. "It's everything. It's the way my whole life is."

"Yeah," Rory says. Her voice is softer. "That's what I thought."

❧ ❧ ❧

A few minutes later, there's a knock on my door.

"Liza." It's Dad talking. He's standing in my doorway, and he's practically yelling my name. Everything sounds louder than it is usually. "Liza, Mom and I want you and Jane to come downstairs. We need to talk to you."

I haven't seen Dad since he got angry at me yesterday. He looks terrible. He probably looks even worse than I do. His face is pale and his eyes are red-rimmed. Usually, he's like a force of nature—so much energy and spirit that it almost knocks you over. But not today. He looks like a wilted cornstalk, hanging on to the door so he won't fall down.

"I'll be there in a minute," I say. He nods and leaves. I can hear him knocking on Jane's door, down the hall.

I stand up. I'm feeling a little better, but not much. I need to be alone. I don't need to move.

I've already been up for an hour and now I want to stay in bed. I want to lie here and think of all the ways I've ruined my life. Maybe I'll even cry again. Before yesterday, I hadn't cried in years, because it's not good for me. But maybe I will today.

But anyway, I want to be by myself, with all the doors closed and shades down and phones turned off. Except people won't leave me alone.

Downstairs, Mom and Dad and Jane are sitting around the dining room table. Even Granddad's there. He looks as confused as I am. "You sick, hon?" he asks me when I sit down next to him.

Mom clears her throat. "I want to talk to all of you about something very important," she says. "I have decided . . . I have decided that I am not going ahead with the stem-cell transplant."

I sit there and watch the grain of wood in the dining room table—how it swirls and swoops and curls. If I look up, I know I'll see all the same, familiar pictures in the dining room—the painting of a woman's back, the framed map of the Republic of Texas, the painting of a blue-and-green landscape. If I look farther to my left, I know I'll see the kitchen. To the right is the living room. Everything's where it's always been. Everything's the same. Everything is here.

But it's not. Something's happened, and nothing is the same. Everything is stopped and frozen in the room. I'm not sure I can even breathe in here, because my body is frozen, too. I can't hear anything. Not the wind or the hum of the refrigerator or the cat outside. Nothing. There's no sound. Except for Jane's crying.

I take my eyes off the table and look at Mom. For just a few seconds, I stare straight into her eyes, the way I did yesterday. Her eyes are so blue, like they're made of crystal. That's how they've always been—beautiful and wide and innocent. But there's something different about them now. They're stronger and steadier than they used to be.

Why? What is it? What happened?

It's like Dad said. She's seeing things we don't see. Is that what's going on? What's she seeing that I don't understand? How did I miss something this important? Things are happening all around me, to me, with me. But I haven't even noticed them. Not in the way they should be noticed. I thought I knew what was going on, but I didn't. I've missed everything, somehow. Everything important.

I look at Dad. He's sitting right beside Mom, and she has her arm around his shoulder. He's slumped and he's looking down. He isn't looking at any of us. I watch while Mom touches him and strokes his hair. I wish I could stop watching. It doesn't seem right. They should be alone if they're doing things like that.

"Mom—are you going to die?" Jane asks.

Her words expand till they're filling the whole room, like a fog you've never seen before, but now it's wrapping itself around you, squeezing hard, squeezing the breath out of you till you're gasping and panicked. Is Mom going to die? No, she isn't. Of course, she isn't. We don't talk like that in our family. We don't, because we don't need to. Things like that don't happen to us.

197

"Am I going to die?" Mom's voice is soft, but firm. "Oh, babe, of course I'm going to die. We're all going to die, sooner or later.

"But I'm not going to die before I live some more and we spend more time together and we try to discuss every damned thing in the world I think is important. I'm not going to let you grow up without me. I'm going to be here for both you girls for as long as I can. I want to leave you both with what's best about me. I want you to know that I'll always be with you."

"But, Mom—*why?*" I ask. My voice is shaking so hard, I barely recognize it. "If you love us, why aren't you going to go through with the stem-cell transplant? *Don't you want to live?*"

Dad makes a noise. He sounds like he's crying. Mom moves her hand over his. For a few seconds, she stares at their hands and doesn't say anything. Then she lifts her head.

"I do want to live," she says. "That isn't what this is about, Lizzie. I'm going to consider other treatments. But I just don't want to live the way I'd have to live with a stem-cell transplant—bald and weak and drugged and desperately sick—feeling so bad that I'm not even myself anymore. Looking so bad that people I love don't even recognize me. Losing every bit of dignity I have.

"And for what? For a small chance of living longer?" She stops, then her voice gets louder. "I won't do it. I will not do it. That's not life to me. That's not anything I care about. Can you understand what I'm saying? I won't live that way.

"Everyone wants me to do it. Your father . . . my doctors . . . you girls . . . friends and neighbors. Everyone wants me to do it. . . . Everyone says I should fight it . . . except for some of my friends who are breast cancer survivors. No one else understands right now. No one else wants to talk to me about what *I* want to do . . . and how scared I am sometimes. No one . . . no one wants me to talk about all these dark places that are so real to me. No one."

She stops talking, and we all sit there quietly. Mom seems tired after everything she's said, and Jane and I don't say anything. Neither does Dad. Granddad is staring out the window. I wonder if he's heard anything.

Mom still has her hand on Dad's, and she leans over to kiss him. Watching them, I feel older and younger, all at the same time. I don't understand anything right now. Maybe I never understood anything. I just thought I did. Everything I knew—about Mom and Dad, about myself, about Richard, about every damned thing on earth—has been wrong. It makes me feel stupid for the first time in my life. I'm not as smart as I thought I was. That's clear. I didn't understand as much as I thought I did.

Dad had taught me so much, and we thought we knew everything. We thought we were the strong ones—but maybe we were wrong. Or maybe we were strong for a while, and then everything shifted and changed, and we couldn't recognize anything or anybody because they weren't the same. Maybe Mom's the one who's been seeing things as they really are. And not us, because we couldn't do it. We couldn't go on.

We thought we'd been protecting her for years. That's what Dad had told me, and that's what I'd thought. But maybe it wasn't nearly that simple.

God, how could I have been so dumb? Right now, sitting at this small wood table that we're gathered around, I wonder how much Mom's protected me without my knowing it.

How could I have missed that for so long?

❦ ❦ ❦

The next day, Mom and Jane and I take an afternoon drive. Dad must not have told Mom about my wreck, because she wants me to drive. I'm kind of relieved by that. I thought nobody would ever want me to drive again, ever. I'd have to take taxis everywhere, which is very hard to do when you live in a place like Austin, where there are only about three taxis in the whole city.

"Take Mopac south," Mom says.

That's the freeway close to our house. It's also the freeway where I had my wreck. I wonder if it's where Deborah Ames had her wreck, too. I've never been sure where that happened.

I pull the car onto the freeway pretty smoothly. After I've been there for five minutes without crashing into anybody, I feel a lot better. I check in the rearview mirror and turn on my signal indicator and change lanes. If you didn't know what a horrible driving history I have and how I flunked driver's ed, you might think I'm an okay driver. I wonder if I should tell Mom and Jane what happened. They might not want to risk their lives like this. They've always thought I was the safe, stable, responsible type. Maybe I should let them know I'm not.

"Take the next exit and go right," Mom says.

It's the road to Fredericksburg, and it goes through the Hill Country, winding through green fields and small, quiet towns, along the side of ranches and farms. At least it used to be like that. Now, you can see giant, sprawling new houses on the tops of the hills and newer cars and trucks, and faces that aren't as brown and weatherbeaten. Granddad says that a lot of people who have moved here wouldn't know a horse if it took a dump on their heads. He's especially upset because a lot of the people who've moved here are Yankees. Sometimes Granddad talks about the Civil War so much, you'd think he actually fought in it.

We come to the top of a hill, and the view is beautiful, with rolling land that looks almost like a brown-and-green ocean that spreads all the way to the horizon. It's beautiful, but it makes me feel dizzy to look at it. It reminds me of the view from Mount Bonnell the other night with Richard.

I pull into the artists' fair we're going to, and Jane and Mom and I spend the rest of the afternoon walking from stand to stand in the tents. We see dream-catchers from New Mexico—hoops and nets that are decorated with soft feathers. We see black-and-white photographs of rural Texas roads and rows and rows of brightly colored jewelry. We see ceramic pots and vivid, shiny materials and carved wooden figures of cowboys and windmills—the way life used to be here.

We stop in a tent with a big oven and eat barbecue sandwiches that drip grease on the butcher paper and down our chins. Mom pushes napkins toward us. That's what she always does when we eat out. She always gets us too many napkins.

Then, finally, after the sun is down, we get back in the car. Before we've driven a few miles, Jane's fallen asleep in the backseat. Her head's propped against the seat, and her hair is spilling out on her shoulders, like sheets of bright, copper pennies. For some reason, she looks even younger than she is, like she's still a little girl.

"My baby," Mom says. "She's still my baby. Do you know how much she admires you, Liza?"

It's quiet in the car, so I ask Mom a question I've always wanted to ask. "Why did you stop writing? Why did you just—well, give up?"

"Oh, that," Mom says. "I haven't thought about it in ages. I stopped writing because I wasn't that good, babe. I didn't have a voice—that's what everyone said. And they were right. I didn't have a voice." She runs her hand through her hair and laughs, for some reason. "It's the strangest thing, Liza. Sometimes I think I've found it. Finally."

We drive through the hills and trees, and Mom keeps on talking. She talks about being diagnosed with cancer. Her words come out quickly and softly.

"It's the worst thing you can be told—that you have cancer," she says. "That's what everyone thinks. But it's not. It's something terrible and beautiful and painful. I . . . I don't know if I can explain this well enough . . . to make you understand, babe."

We both sit in the car for about a minute, then Mom starts to talk again. "I used to be so scared of everything . . . of life. And now I'm not. I'm sick. I know that. I'll probably die from this disease—but it may not be for years. It's hard for everybody else to understand, but being sick has freed me, somehow. I know I'm going to die from this eventually, but I'm freer than I've ever been in my life.

"I can't explain it any better than that, Lizzie."

I reach out and touch her hand. It's soft and white and warm. Right now, it's alive. It can move and touch me back and stroke my cheek, the way it's doing now. How long will that last? For just a few seconds, I wonder what life will be like without Mom. But I shake my head and try to fling it away. I can't think about that now. I will soon. I will someday. But right now, this minute, I can't.

"Sometimes," Mom says, "I feel as if I've been picked up and shaken and thrown back down to earth. And now I have to put things back together. And you know what? Maybe it's not a bad thing to be shaken like that." She turns and pats my cheek and gives me a kiss. I can feel her warm breath on me.

"Mom—what was your book about? You never told me."

She smiles. "My book? Do you really want to know?"

So she tells me the story she burned a few years ago in our fireplace. The miles pass, and I listen as carefully as I can. I'm trying to remember what she says, trying to understand everything I've missed.

The scenery whips by us, big black trees by the side of the road that winds up and down hills, past fences and barns and herds of cattle. We're plunging into the darkness and the damp air, racing along the road, feeling the wind whip into the windows. As fast as we're going, we should be home soon.

202

Both Sides Now

Now

BY RUTH PENNEBAKER

A READERS GUIDE

★ *"Ultimately hopeful and realistic."*
—SCHOOL LIBRARY JOURNAL, Starred

QUESTIONS FOR DISCUSSION

1. Rebecca and Liza have different ideas and feelings about breast cancer. Rebecca wants her family to see the changes in her personality and the ways in which she is stronger now. Liza is afraid to talk about her mother's illness. Discuss the reasons for these different responses. How would you feel?

2. Liza feels anxious when her mother talks about cancer. Liza describes the "panic rising . . . like a siren that's going off" and the need to stop her mother from elaborating on her fear of dying. (p. 138) Why do you think Liza resists these discussions?

3. How would you describe Liza's reaction in the wig store? Why is she afraid to lose control of her emotions?

4. Rebecca describes Liza as "holding on too tight, trying to hold on to something that's not there any longer." (p. 132) How are Liza's actions affecting her emotionally?

5. What function do the characters of Richard, Mr. Sorenson, Rory, Emma, and Beverly serve in the story? How do they represent part of Liza's other world, outside her home life?

6. When Rebecca tells her family she does not want the stem-cell transplant, Liza realizes, "We thought we'd been protecting her for years. That's what Dad had told me, and that's what I'd thought. But maybe it wasn't nearly that simple. . . . I wonder how much Mom's protected me without my knowing it." (p. 199) What does Liza recognize now about her mother's strength of spirit?

7. "I feel as if I've been picked up and shaken and thrown back down to earth. And now I have to put things back together." (p. 202) What do you think of Rebecca's description of her experience as a breast cancer survivor? How does this relate to Liza's feelings?

8. How does the ending make you feel? Discuss the ways Liza and Rebecca are better equipped to talk with each other after honestly discussing breast cancer.

9. Do you know someone with breast cancer? Have you ever discussed your family history?

In her own words—
a conversation with
RUTH PENNEBAKER

James Pennebaker

A CONVERSATION WITH RUTH PENNEBAKER

Q. What prompted you to write *Both Sides Now*?

A. Nothing is more fascinating to me than how a family works—or doesn't work. I wanted to write a novel about a loving family that has lived well and happily together for years, but then something extraordinarily difficult happens—a recurrence of breast cancer, in this case—and the way the family has lived no longer works. Under dramatically altered circumstances, the four of them have to change and re-create themselves if they are going to survive. The father, who has always been the "strong" one in the family under more ordinary circumstances, finds himself lost and ineffectual. It's the mother, who may well die from breast cancer, who finds a certain strength and freedom that she's never had before, and is able to help her husband and their two children face what is real—as opposed to what they want reality to be.

Q. The discussions between Liza and Rebecca, her mother, are very poignant. Did you find inspiration for them in your own experiences with your children?

A. No, unfortunately. My daughter, who was thirteen when I was diagnosed with breast cancer in 1995, now says her father and I thought we were open with her and her brother, but we weren't. I'm sure she's right. We were so overwhelmed by the diagnosis, then by the treatments (surgery, reconstructive surgery, chemotherapy, and radiation), that it was all we could do to function minimally. It's often difficult for a mother and teenage daughter to communicate under good circumstances, and having a life-threatening illness can undermine even the best efforts to talk to your kids. But the sense that Liza and Rebecca keep missing each other, trying to communicate but failing, is as much about any mother-daughter relationship as it is about the travails of breast cancer.

Q. Whom do you see as your audience for this novel?

A. Families who have been touched by life-threatening illness, either in their own midst or through their friends. I think it would be helpful for women diagnosed with an illness, as well as their teenagers. When you're in the middle of such a tremendous crisis, I think it would be helpful in encouraging you to think about the other members of your family and how they are all trying—however unsuccessfully—to handle both illness and the possibility of death.

Q. Rebecca describes her cancer as "a part of my body that's reeled out of control—wild, extravagant cells that multiply and refuse to die. It's a part of me, whether I like it or not. I can't hate it the way I need to hate it." (p. 52) Is this description something you imagined, or do you think cancer survivors feel this way?

A. People have different ways of handling and visualizing what they're going through. Some of them use the imagery of battle—talking about going to war against cancer, fighting it, and hating it. I never felt comfortable with that. The cancer was a part of my body, and I didn't or couldn't hate it. It was a shadow in my life and my body, and I was incapable of hating that shadow. (Go figure.)

When I was going through treatment, my husband and I saw the movie *Jeffrey*, which was based on Paul Rudnik's play of the same name. At one point in the movie, some thugs jump Jeffrey and the question is asked: What weapons does he bring to this particular fight? "I have irony," Jeffrey says. I loved that and identified with it completely. I had irony, too.

Q. Liza and Rebecca are the main voices in *Both Sides Now*. Did you plan the novel with this in mind, or did the two voices come together as you were writing?

A. I'm not the biggest planner in the world. Originally, the book was all in Liza's voice, and my editor suggested something that would bring the reader closer to Rebecca's experience. I think that was a great idea. I wanted Rebecca to be able to speak for herself—and not merely through Liza. Too, that allowed me to show how distant the two were from each other, especially at the beginning of the book.

Q. What do you think of the portrayal of breast cancer in the media? Is there greater awareness, or do we have to increase the focus on this issue?

A. You know, I think there's plenty of focus on breast cancer these days, thanks to some very brave women like Betty Ford and Nancy Brinker. But I do quibble with the media's focus on it, especially every October. The stories are invariably perky and upbeat, with the message that early detection will save your life. That's true in many cases—but not all. There are many different forms of breast cancer, and some are so aggressive that even early detection won't stop them. Breast cancer still kills, and not all the stories are upbeat.

Q. What can someone do to get involved in the fight against breast cancer? What are the volunteer organizations, etc., that need our help?

A. Most communities have a Race for the Cure in the fall, which is a good way to increase awareness of breast cancer and raise money for research. That helps tremendously, as well as informing yourself as much as you can about the disease, its signs, and the latest treatments for it.

Q. Rebecca worries that she's caused her daughters to feel *"like traitors—because they're sexual and healthy and whole and I'm not. . . . Or as if they're doomed. . . . As if we're all doomed, somehow, for being women."* (p. 94) Why did you write that sentence? Do you believe women are "doomed" by breast cancer, or is Rebecca's illness affecting her thoughts?

A. No, I don't think women are "doomed" by being female or getting breast cancer, but it is a peculiarly female disease (although one out of every 100 diagnoses is a male). I wrote that sentence because of something I read—that it was particularly hard on girls who were entering adolescence when their mothers were diagnosed with a disease that is primarily identified as a female's disease and centers on a part of the body that is a symbol of womanhood. It seemed to me that that would be very confusing and troubling to a girl who is already at such a confusing time in her life. What happens to her natural delight in her own growing breasts under these circumstances? It has to be enormously difficult.

Q. Do you have a message to young women today? What advice would you give them?

A. One reason I wanted to write this book is that I do have problems with the whole attitude-is-everything cult these days. I usually refer to these people as the Optimism Police. When you're diagnosed with cancer, they bombard you with advice about having a great attitude and you, too, will survive. That's garbage—not to mention a blame-the-victim game. I've known far too many women with superb and positive attitudes who moved heaven and earth to live but died nevertheless. I think it's both normal and healthy to feel sad and angry about getting cancer. Why wouldn't you? Who wants to have an iron-on smile and have a philosophy of life brief and simplistic enough to put on a T-shirt?

So that would be my message: More than anything, people with cancer should be allowed to express everything they're feeling and not be shamed into silence if their attitudes aren't sufficiently uplifting. There is no one way to go through all of this. We all do it differently and we all do the best we can.

Q. How has being a breast cancer survivor changed your opinion, attitude, and outlook on life?

A. When I thought I was going to die, I was scared—but I also had a tremendous sense of clarity about what was important in my life. I valued that clarity and the sense that I had to clear away everything that wasn't truly important. My family, my friends, and my work were what was most important to me, and I try to retain that sense of clarity. Love and work—those are the most important things in my life. It's not a bad thing to have been so profoundly shaken by something that you have to evaluate your entire life; I felt driven to wring every possible bit of good and meaning out of the whole terrible experience. Even now, six years later, I have a greater sense of urgency about my time on this earth—and I don't regret that urgency. Don't wait. Don't count on an endless future. Say the things that you don't want to die without saying. Let the people you love know that you love them.

National Breast Cancer Foundation, Inc.

The official site for the national organization, with the latest news and medical updates.

www.nationalbreastcancer.org

National Breast Cancer Coalition

The National Breast Cancer Coalition is a grassroots advocacy effort in the fight against breast cancer.

www.natlbcc.org

National Alliance of Breast Cancer Organizations

A user-friendly site with a list of local and national groups, a calendar of events, and research information.

www.nabco.org

A Ring of Endless Light
MADELEINE L'ENGLE
0-440-97232-9
Fifteen-year-old Vicky Austin
spends a difficult summer confronting
the problems of first love and the slow
death of her grandfather.

Bone Dance
MARTHA BROOKS
0-440-22791-7
When seventeen-year-old Alexandra
inherits a rural cabin from the father she
never knew, she meets Lonny, a boy also
torn by grief and visions he can't shake.

Stone Water
BARBARA SNOW GILBERT
0-440-22755-0
Grant Hughes's beloved grandfather
asks Grant to help him die if he is
transferred to the terminal ward of the
nursing home.

Kit's Wilderness
DAVID ALMOND
0-440-41605-1

Kit Watson and John Askew look for the childhood ghosts of their long-gone ancestors in the mines of Stoneygate.

Skellig
DAVID ALMOND
0-440-22908-1

Michael feels helpless because of his baby sister's illness, until he meets a creature called Skellig.

Heaven Eyes
DAVID ALMOND
0-440-22910-3

Erin Law and her friends in the orphanage are labeled Damaged Children. They run away one night, traveling downriver on a raft. What they find on their journey is stranger than you can imagine.
Available October 2002

Becoming Mary Mehan: Two Novels
JENNIFER ARMSTRONG
0-440-22961-8

Set against the events of the American Civil War, *The Dreams of Mairhe Mehan* depicts an Irish immigrant girl and her family, who are struggling to find their place in the war-torn country. *Mary Mehan Awake* takes up Mary's story after the war, when she must begin a journey of renewal.

Forgotten Fire
ADAM BAGDASARIAN
0-440-22917-0

In 1915, Vahan Kenderian is living a life of privilege when his world is shattered by the Turkish-Armenian war.

Ghost Boy
IAIN LAWRENCE
0-440-41668-X

Fourteen-year-old Harold Kline is an albino—an outcast. When the circus comes to town, Harold runs off to join it in hopes of discovering who he is and what he wants in life. Is he a circus freak or just a normal guy?

The Giver
LOIS LOWRY
0-440-23768-8

Jonas's world is perfect. Everything is under control. There is no war or fear or pain. There are no choices, until Jonas is given an opportunity that will change his world forever.
Available September 2002

Gathering Blue
LOIS LOWRY
0-440-22949-9

Lamed and suddenly orphaned, Kira is mysteriously removed to live in the palatial Council Edifice, where she is expected to use her gifts as a weaver to do the bidding of the all-powerful Guardians.
Available September 2002

Both Sides Now
RUTH PENNEBAKER
0-440-22933-2

A compelling look at breast cancer through the eyes of a mother and daughter. Liza must learn a few life lessons from her mother, Rebecca, about the power of family.

Her Father's Daughter
MOLLIE POUPENEY
0-440-22879-4
As she matures from a feisty tomboy of seven to a spirited young woman of fourteen, Maggie discovers that the only constant in her life of endless new homes and new faces is her ever-emerging sense of herself.

The Baboon King
ANTON QUINTANA
0-440-22907-3
Neither Morengáru's father's Masai tribe nor his mother's Kikuyu tribe accepts him. Banished from both tribes, Morengáru encounters a baboon troop and faces a fight with the simian king.

Holes
LOUIS SACHAR
0-440-22859-X
Stanley has been unjustly sent to a boys' detention center, Camp Green Lake. But there's more than character improvement going on at the camp—the warden is looking for something.

Memories of Summer
RUTH WHITE
0-440-22921-9
In 1955, thirteen-year-old Lyric describes her older sister Summer's descent into mental illness, telling Summer's story with humor, courage, and love.

DATE DUE

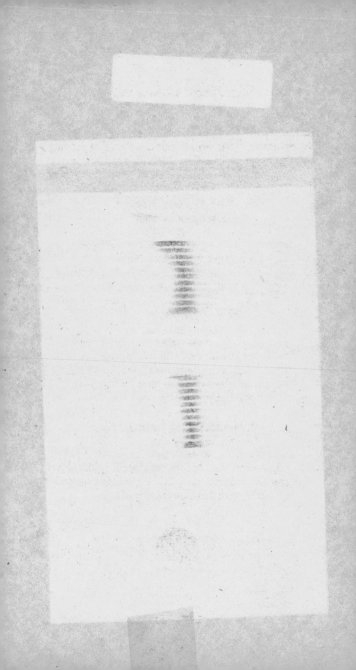